TEARDROPS AND FLIP FLOPS

A Laugh Out Loud Romantic Comedy about a Traveling Widow, Her Rescue Dog, and the Men Who Want to Court Them.

LARK GRIFFING

WIND LARK
PUBLISHING

ISBN-13: 978-0-9988719-4-3

Edited by Wing Family Editing

Cover Design by Wicked Whale Publishing

For my husband, Joe,
the man who built my teardrop
and always allows me to follow my heart.

Part One

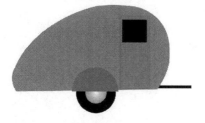

Chapter 1

Ruby chewed on the end of her pen, concentrating on her newest list. Retirement. George looked over and noticed her scowl. He studied her for a moment, and his heart swelled with love. This woman, his woman, he loved her the moment he set eyes on her so many years ago. She was fiery and stubborn, and full of adventure. So different from him. He remembered the first time he saw her. She stood on the top of a bale of straw, her hands on her hips, her auburn hair shining copper in the sun. She was barking orders to two young men, telling them where to move the other bales in order to set the stage for the photographs of the children. Ruby was in charge, and she would be damned if it wasn't going to be perfect. He jumped in and followed her every direction. She leaned on him, and he made things happen. Everything fell into place from there.

That was their senior year in college. They dated for six months, he proposed, she said yes, and that was that. He always knew she was just comfortable with him. He suspected she loved him but wasn't in love with him. George was sorry she missed that in her life, but he had it, and he loved every day of it.

She scowled again and jotted something else on her list; a sea green three by five card charged with keeping her world in order. She had a stack of them next to her chair, color coded, regulated to different aspects of her life. Her life, not what she expected, he knew that. She yearned for adventure; he yearned for family. Neither of them got their wish. All her dreams of adventure buried under her work load, and his dreams of children, dashed by infertility.

"Why are you scowling? What is it that makes that pretty face of yours look sad?"

"I was just thinking."

"That's what I was afraid of. You thinking often equals me working." He smiled at her indulgently, remembering the brick walkway she was 'just thinking about' one day that took him three weekends and then a call to a landscaper to finish. He just wasn't the handy type.

"I was thinking about when we retire. What we can do."

"We can do anything we want. Just name it. I am at your service." He figured she would want to get a condo somewhere on a beach or maybe cruise around Panama. That wasn't his idea of a good time. He was a homebody and would rather stay in his easy chair and watch the most recent loss of his favorite Cleveland sports team.

"I want to buy a trailer and travel the country, living like gypsies. Wouldn't that be awesome?" Ruby turned and looked at him, her eyebrows raised in excitement, her beautiful green eyes flashing with a quest for adventure.

George groaned inwardly. Here we go again, he thought. Five years ago, it was the Appalachian Trail. Two years ago, it was the Camino de Santiago. She dreamed, she read, she watched videos. Of course, it didn't happen. It never did. Time didn't allow such dalliances. At least this time, it didn't involve walking hundreds, perhaps thousands of miles. He smiled brightly at her and made a noncommittal guttural noise.

Ruby sighed. She knew that sound. That was George's way of humoring her without starting an argument. She knew he would never go for her idea. Sure, he would placate her, maybe even go to an RV show with her to feed her dream, but deep inside he would hope for her to move on to the next idea, the next imagined adventure. If he waited long enough, she would. He thought it was because she eventually lost interest in the idea. The truth was, she just gave up. She knew when things were hopeless. She had learned that during her early years, those tender, formative years of childhood. That part of her was bottled up tightly, never to see the light of day. George just figured she was flighty, moving from one set of dreams to another. What he didn't know was she figured out a long time ago when to cut her losses.

Ruby chewed her pen some more and added to the list: Assateague Island, Mount Washington, Newfound Gap, Canyon of the Ancients… all the places she had dreamed of seeing or had read about when she was a kid, using her imagination to escape the special kind of horror that only she knew.

George understood when he had to make an accommodating move. He put down his newspaper and peered over his cheaters.

"So, what's on your list? Different kinds of travel trailer things?" he asked, trying hard to feign interest. He knew better though. She knew him inside and out. There was no fooling her. "Okay, seriously, I could think about it. What, you want to be like those people we saw on the TV the other night, the ones who sold everything and lived in their motor home?"

"No," Ruby laughed at the thought of George leaving his beloved chair and giant TV to travel in a house on wheels. "I couldn't torture you that much. I was thinking more like traveling a few weeks at a time, seeing the country, and then coming home so you could, you know, decompress, or something." She smiled, encouraging him to warm to the idea. "But, there are so many places I want to see. I mean, I love the vacations we've taken. The Caribbean cruise was very nice, and D.C. in spring, with all those cherry blossoms were beautiful, but traveling the open road, going wherever we want, whenever we want would be amazing." With that, Ruby scribbled two more places on her mint green index card; Juneau, Alaska and Banff, Canada.

"I think that sounds ... interesting, dear," said George with as much enthusiasm as he could muster. "You work on your ideas and let me know what you think. I'm going to take a shower and turn in early. It was a hard day at the office today, and I'm feeling tired." George rose and tenderly kissed his wife of twenty-four years on the top of the head. Her hair was silky and warm. "We've got time to plan. We won't be retiring any time soon," sighed George as he contemplated the next nineteen years of working at the accounting firm. Most people would find that idea frightening, Ruby certainly would, but he found comfort in the routine. Order was his mantra.

He climbed the stairs thinking he felt so tired that night. Not good. Not good at all. As he turned the corner, he looked one last time lovingly at his wife, his angel. It was okay that she didn't love him with the passion that he felt for her. He just felt lucky to have her in his life. But a travel trailer? The thought pained him.

Chapter 2

R uby had a hard time concentrating. She was editing an article about the horror of tan lines, and she just wasn't feeling it. Usually she enjoyed the weird things she learned when she edited. The company she worked for provided writing and editing services, and she worked on everything from textbooks to magazine articles. Not only did her job provide her with a living wage, but Ruby was now an expert on the proper way of rolling on a condom with panache, making the perfect Mojito, and historic myths about our founding fathers that don't hold water. Overall, the condom article was one of her favorites, although obtaining semen from a prize race horse for artificial insemination was a close second.

Despite the fascinating tan line dilemma, Ruby's thoughts kept wandering to life on the road in a camper. It had been three weeks since she had first broached the subject to George. Once, over a particularly fine meal of Beef Wellington at the Greenland Tavern, she tried again, regaling him with information about trailers that sported recliners and an outdoor TV. George tried to be enthusiastic, but the Wellington had left his stomach queasy, and he had spent the evening popping Tums.

The ringing of her phone interrupted her musing, and she reached absently for it.

"Hello. This is Ruby, how may I help you?"

"Ruby, it's Tom. I'm sorry…"

"Tom? Why are you calling me? What's going on?" There was an awkward silence. The sound of a clearing throat. "Is something wrong with George? Oh God, Tom. What happened?"

"Ruby, you have to get to General right away. They've taken him by ambulance. I think it's his heart. I'm so sorry, Ruby. If there is anything I can do… anything the firm can do. Please let me know."

R uby burst through the elevator doors, looking around wildly for anyone to help her. A woman in blue scrubs covered with happy, puppy dog faces cupped Ruby's elbow with her hand and gently guided her to a reception desk.

"My husband. I'm trying to find my husband. They said this floor. I think, his heart."

"What's your name, honey?" asked the woman behind the desk with the expansive bosom and warm, calming smile. "And what is your husband's name?"

"George, his name is George. George Dunning. I'm Ruby. His wife. Ruby." Her hands flew to her hair, trying to pat down the flyaways, vaguely aware she might be disheveled.

"Ah, here he is, George Dunning. They are getting him ready for surgery right now. I have some paperwork for you." The woman with the comforting soft curves glanced behind Ruby, catching the slight shake of the head from the dog scrub lady. Ruby caught the exchange.

"Wait. What? What's wrong? Surgery?"

The cheerful puppy once again took Ruby's elbow and led her down the hall. She began to speak in a quiet comforting voice.

"Your husband has had heart issues. He is being prepped for surgery. I don't know if I can get a doctor to speak with you just now, they are getting prepared, but I will see what I can do." She guided Ruby to a hard, orange plastic chair situated by a glossy, wide leaf plant and a contemporary painting of an angel, or maybe a flock of birds, it was hard to tell.

A set of double doors burst open and a gurney rumbled toward them at a quick pace. Ruby followed puppy scrub's gaze and realized her George was on that gurney. She jumped up from the chair and ran to his side. The gurney didn't stop.

"George. I love you, George. You're going to be okay. You have to be okay." She was running to keep up. George reached his hand toward hers and smiled a tired smile at her worried face.

"Don't worry, sweetheart. I've had the happiest years of my life with you. It's all good."

"Don't talk like that, George. The doctors will fix it. I promise. I know they will."

"Hush, Ruby. Listen. I want you to be happy. I want you to always be happy. Promise me that."

"I am happy. George you make me happy. I love you."

"I know you, Ruby. I know your heart. Get my things from my desk at work..."

"Excuse me," interrupted an efficient looking doctor with the most startling blue, cold eyes. "I need to get this man into my operating room."

"This man is my husband, and I love him, and I want to know what is going on."

"If I stop to explain this all to you, he won't be around to love."

Ruby gasped in surprise, not expecting the brusque manner or the cold, hard reality of his words.

"Ruby, I love you. I think this is my last stop. I bought you a…" and with that George's eyes closed, and the medical crew whisked him away. Puppy scrubs grabbed Ruby and barred her from following them.

Chapter 3

Ruby closed the front door and leaned against it, George's belongings stuffed in a bag dangled from her wrist. The house seemed unnaturally quiet. She didn't move. She didn't know what to do. It was over so quickly. There wasn't even time for the surgery. One minute he was talking to her, the next minute his eyes were closed, and he was gone.

She had no idea how long she stood there. It may have been five minutes, it may have been thirty, but she didn't move. She just closed her eyes and didn't move. Like if she didn't move, then the world wouldn't shatter around her. Like if she didn't move, everything would hold together. Like if she didn't move, George would still be here, still smiling, still breathing, still freaking living. The minutes ticked by. The bag on her wrist grew heavier. The light shifted in the foyer as the sun changed position. The minutes ticked by. The. Minutes. Ticked. By.

The doorbell rang, sending Ruby into flight. She jumped away from the door and looked around her as if she didn't know where she was. The doorbell rang again. She turned and opened it, bracing herself for whoever was on the other side. A perky little girl with shiny, straight cut bangs and a perky pink headband shoved a box of cookies at her. Ruby stared at her, registering the fact that the perky pink headband looked out of place with the uniform she was wearing.

"Ya wanna buy some cookies?" The girl beamed at her, showing off her perfectly matched set of missing front teeth. "Just four dollars a box. How many do you want?" She stood there, staring at Ruby expectantly.

Ruby reached into the plastic bag still dangling from her wrist. She pulled ten dollars out of her dead husband's wallet, handed it to the girl, then turned and closed the door. The girl stood, staring at the door. Shrugging her shoulders, she set two boxes of cookies on the porch and carefully counted out two dollars change. She set the change on the boxes. A soft breeze blew them off, and they floated to the porch floor. She bent over and plucked the bills off the porch and tucked them under the boxes. Satisfied she ran down the sidewalk waving the ten-dollar bill at her mom who was waiting in the car, staring at her cell phone.

Chapter 4

I took the liberty of having Jenny box up George's things. I'm sorry… it sounds so harsh. I really don't know what to say."

"It's okay, Tom. I appreciate everything you and the firm have done. You are so kind." Ruby stared helplessly at the two cardboard boxes, the testament to her husband's years at the accounting firm.

"Take your time in here. There's no hurry. Just have Jenny buzz me when you are ready, and I'll get a couple of the guys help you carry the boxes to your car." Tom paused, searching her eyes. Ruby was touched by the kindness and the depth of sadness there. "Ruby, take a few minutes in here. This was such a part of his life. Take all the time in the world." He squeezed her right shoulder. Absently, she lifted her hand to cover his. They stayed. In that moment. Remembering a truly good man. Tom turned and left, closing the door softly behind him.

Ruby walked to the desk. George's desk. The boxes were loaded with the odds and ends a desk collects when it is part of a busy work life. Not just the pens and pencils, but the favorite boss coffee mugs, and the mustache sticky notes Ruby jokingly bought George one year. Joke's on us, she thought. She reached in and picked up a strange looking blue ball with tunnels bored through. It was soft and slightly sticky, but not unpleasantly so. She squeezed it. A loud, obscene, wet, farting, crackling sound burst from her fist. Unexpected laughter escaped her lips. Tears streamed down her cheeks as she hiccupped loudly, caught in the wild space between laughter and hysterical sadness.

The door opened.

"Ruby? Honey are you okay?" Jenny, George's admin hesitantly crossed the plush carpet, closing the distance between them, but not knowing if she should.

"It's okay, Jenny. I just found this." Ruby gave the ball a hearty squeeze and the wet sound ripped through the air. Jenny looked surprised, but saw the smile on Ruby's lips, so she relaxed and laughed quietly,

"That was George's favorite desk toy, at least it was after Tom took the rocket launcher away from him." Ruby looked up, searching Jenny's face.

"Rocket launcher?"

"Yeah, it was from the *Desks of Destruction* website. That was his favorite place to shop. The rocket launcher could send pencils all the way across the office. Once he was annoyed with Tom. Tom was riding him about something. When Tom turned to leave, George shot him in the ass with a brand-new number two. Tom confiscated the toy. George said he felt violated. Tom gave him the stress ball to make up for it. They were great friends." She smiled a wistful, sympathetic smile. "Ruby, we will miss him so much."

Ruby shrugged her shoulders in a helpless thanks.

"That was insensitive of me," said Jenny. "Of course, you will miss him more. I didn't mean to…"

"For the love of God, stop being so freaking socially aware. It's me, Jenny. Please…" Ruby's voice trailed off as she found she couldn't put the thoughts into words. "Let me try that again, please. I appreciate your words. Everyone loved George. He was one of the kindest men I know. I am pretty sure everyone will have a hole in their life because he is gone. Yes, my hole is a lot bigger than everyone else's but he was such a good man that I expect that everyone will have that void for a long time. It's nice to know he was so loved."

Jenny wrapped her arms around Ruby, and they held each other, remembering.

Chapter 5

R uby rolled over in bed, absently reaching out to connect, but finding only an empty space. Her heart squeezed as it reminded her that the space next to her would always be empty, the pillow always in the same place, not turned sideways or tossed over her face in the morning, teasing her out of her slumber. She sighed and opened her eyes.

Sunlight was streaming through her window, mocking her with cheerfulness. She groaned. It was Saturday. Saturday. She didn't have to go to work. The day was hers to fill. Every damn freaking minute. Alone.

A phone rang. Startled, she looked around. It wasn't her phone that was ringing. It was George's ring tone. What the hell? She rolled over and plucked the phone off the nightstand on George's side of the bed. It was his personal phone. He never used it because he always used the company phone. She had turned that in to Tom after the funeral.

"Hello?" Ruby asked hesitantly.

"Hello, is George there, please?" an efficient voice asked.

"I'm sorry. He, um isn't available just now." She couldn't bring herself to explain to this stranger that George was dead.

Gone. Isn't available now. Wouldn't ever be again. "Can I help you? I'm his wife."

"Sure. This is Kylie at Sunrise RV. The trailer is still sitting here, and we were wondering when he was going to pick it up. All the paperwork is complete, and it is prepped and ready... Hello?"

Ruby flashed back to the hospital. The last time she saw her husband. Those last minutes. "Ruby, I bought you a..." No. He didn't. Without thinking, she hung up on the speaker. Sliding her slippers on her feet. She grabbed her robe and headed to the dining room. The boxes from the office still sat on the table. Untouched.

She looked inside the cartons and pulled out a handful of file folders. The first one held employment papers, reviews, promotion letters, glowing testimonials from clients. The second held printed copies of website pages. *Desks of Destruction.* George had circled in red new toys he wanted so he could torment Tom.

The last folder held some personal papers. There was a title to a safe deposit box, a shipboard photo of the two of them from their honeymoon cruise, and a flyer from Sunrise RV for the strangest looking trailer she had ever seen. It looked like something from out of the 1920's, a teardrop shape, bright aluminum with shiny red fenders and trim. Sunrise RV. The lady who called. Oh my God. Ruby's heart melted.

Ruby climbed into her Jeep Wrangler. She took a deep breath. Each day presented her with something new. A different sadness. A different heart crushing pain she had to deal with. The first order of business was the safe deposit box. She had forgotten that George had set that up many years ago. She never paid attention to that stuff. George dealt with those details of their life. He was the accountant. Everything in its box, in its place. She was the dreamer. Her life was balanced piles of thoughts and hobbies, to be touched, worked on, then left until it was time to visit again.

The bank verified her identity and helped her access the safe deposit box. She marveled at how George had everything set up for her. She had forgotten all about the box, and her heart pounded as she requested access, but once they checked her license picture and ancient signature, they were satisfied. Inside the box she found a stack of bonds, the deed to the house, several small wrapped presents and a life insurance policy. On top of all these things was a note, written to her.

M*y dearest Ruby,*
Ah honey. How I have loved you. The joy you have given me all of these years has been all I could have hoped for and more. When I was young, I never dreamed I could have had someone as special as you in my life. I fear I have been selfish, though. I have kept you tight to me. Held you by my side. I have always known you have a restless side, a side that needs to explore. You can't sit still, and you can't be settled. I thank you for all the years you have done this for me.

I have had a bad feeling for some time now. My health isn't good. Not that I was keeping this from you, I just didn't want to watch the light inside you flicker and fade. I got to live my time on my terms and not see you deal with any added sadness or pain.

I know a lot more about you than you think. I know what kind of childhood you had. I know why you always feel you need to escape. I wish I could have protected you from that, but I didn't get that opportunity. At least now, I hope I can protect you for the rest of your life. I hope I had time to get everything in order before I pass, but if not, at least you have this. I did some shopping, so I have the next couple of Christmases covered. I know you are not that big on jewelry, but I tried to give you things that would make you smile and remind you of my love. Oh yeah, and I know there is no way you will wait for each Christmas, so go ahead and open them all.

There are bonds for you. I want you to talk to Tom when you are ready. He is prepared to help you navigate the financial part of your life. He was instructed not to bug you for at least a month. If you didn't come to him during that time, then he was going to get with you and go over what you need to know. The life insurance policy is substantial. You should be taken care of for as long as you need. You probably won't have to work if you are careful, but I am pretty sure you will work. I can't imagine you not doing so. Tom will help you with filling out the policy claim if you need help. I don't think you will, but Tom will be there for you. I trust him implicitly. Oh yeah, and when you see him, tell him he can keep my rocket launcher. It's okay, I forgive him.

Ruby, I love you with all my heart. I love you enough to plead with you to be happy. Live your life to the fullest, and if you find someone who shares your wild, restless heart, grab him and don't let him go. Allow yourself to love as fiercely as you can. That is the only regret I have. I think you have never felt that kind of love. Now don't get all defensive on me. I know that you loved me. But I know the truth. You loved me with that comfortable kind of love. That is a very good love. Maybe the best kind. But I wish for you the kind of love that leaves you gasping for breath, that makes your world tilt on its side. This is my wish for you. Remember, I will always be with you. I will always be by your side. I love you forever, my Ruby.

Love, George

R uby rested her head on the table and sobbed. Her body racked with shudders, tears dripping on the paper. Unconscious of the fact that the words were fading with the tears, she cried. When she lifted her head, the salutation was a smeared mess of color. The *love, George* was gone. Her heart shattered.

Chapter 6

"C an I help you?" A silver-haired man in a gray suit reached out his hand to shake Ruby's, but he dropped it quickly when she didn't reciprocate. She wasn't being mean, she was just studying her brochure. He quickly forgave her when he saw she was looking at the Tear 6000, the top of the line retro teardrop trailer. Bert was going to eat well this month. He could feel it in his bones. "Ah, the Tear 6000. The best teardrop trailer out there. Lightweight and efficient, off-road capable, but full of the comforts of home. My name is Bert. Let me show you this beauty."

"I'm sorry. I'm looking for a Kylie Schroeder. Is there a Kylie here?" Ruby asked, scowling down at the business card attached to the brochure.

"Sure, let me see if I can find her." Bert walked to his desk and picked up the phone. He was damn sure not going to find Kylie Schroder. No way. No how. He hung up after fiddling with his phone and looking engaged for a minute, then moved back to Ruby.

"I don't seem to be able to reach her at her desk. Maybe she is out on the lot or at lunch. Please, I am certain I can help you and answer any questions about this beautiful little trailer." He continued to move her toward a turquoise blue retro-style trailer in the middle of the showroom floor.

"You must be Ruby." A young woman purposely strode past Bert. His shoulders slumped, and he murmured something about seeing him if they needed anything. He slunk off to the coffee machine.

"Yes, I am Ruby. You're Kylie? You called me this morning?" asked Ruby. Kylie nodded her head enthusiastically. "How did you know my name? How did you know what I looked like?"

"George was so excited to get this trailer for you. He talked non-stop about you, what you liked, what you looked like. He showed me a picture of you in his wallet. You were standing on top of a cliff at the edge of a waterfall. George said he couldn't bring himself to go up there with you, but he loved this picture. He said it caught your daring essence. He couldn't wait for this trailer to be ready. He said he wanted to surprise you. He was supposed to pick it up last week, but he never showed up. He wanted it ready to take you camping this weekend. Are you going to be ready to go? I can't believe he sent you here to get it. Where is he? I know he wanted to watch your face when you saw it." Kylie waited expectantly for Ruby to respond. Ruby swallowed hard, determined to control the tears.

"Yeah, funny thing. He was detained. Couldn't make it today. Had to go, um, out of town. So, he said he wanted me to have this and to go get it. I have no idea, what or how. I know he is disappointed not to be here, but..." her voice trailed off.

"No worries. We will get you set up. He said your Jeep was tow ready and could handle it, right? How cool is it that he just bought you a Wrangler for your trailer? What a super guy you have."

Ruby flashed back to a conversation over dinner. He knew

she always wanted a Wrangler. He took her to the dealership, and she picked out a red one. Red for Ruby. He handled all the details. Tow ready? What did that mean? Although if George said it was tow ready, then she was certain it had to be.

Kylie steered Ruby to her desk and pulled out the paperwork and the keys.

"Oh," Kylie giggled, "I need to see your license to prove you are who you say you are. The trailer is titled to you, so once I see you are Ruby, I can hand over the keys."

The details were taken care of and the delivery paperwork signed. Kylie led Ruby into the back lot. She stopped in front of a beautiful little trailer exactly like the one pictured in the brochure. It shined in the sun, but it was so tiny. When Ruby originally broached the subject of getting a trailer to George, she was thinking of a trailer big enough for him to stretch out every night in a recliner and still feel like he was at home. This was really small. The perfect size for one person. One person. The thought slammed Ruby like a sledge hammer. One person. Her. Without him. Alone.

"Hey, are you okay? Do you like it?"

"I do. I am just overwhelmed. It's very cute. Very tiny."

"That's the beauty of this thing. It's perfect for two people, but one person can move it around and hitch it up easily. It can go anywhere. It doesn't have the limitations of the bigger trailers, and your Jeep can tow it, no problem. It's the perfect solution for one person, or two people who are obviously in love like you and George.

"Okay, let me go over all the details with you. I showed George everything, but he said you were very independent, so I am sure you will want to know how to do everything. After that we'll hook it up to your Jeep and you will be on your way."

They spent the next hour covering all aspects of the trailer. What a gray water tank was, how to empty the black water. Ruby wrinkled her nose at the thought of that. How the side awning worked. Kylie covered everything with ease, but Ruby's head was swimming. Kylie laughed at her and showed her that the manual covered everything in straight forward English. She would be fine.

Ruby backed the Jeep up to the trailer and Kylie showed her how easy it was to hitch up, even for someone as petite as Ruby was.

"Last thing. Have you ever towed anything? Have you ever driven with a trailer behind you?" Ruby shook her head. "Okay. Then just take it slowly. Give lots of room to move over and change lanes. Keep your speed down, and remember that you have another ten feet or so behind you that is occupied by a trailer. Oh, and go to an empty parking lot and practice backing up. It can be tricky. I'd have you do it here, but we have too many RV's in our lots. There is an abandoned super-store a few miles south of here. Stay on this road. You can't miss it. Practice there for a while until you get the hang of it. Any other questions? If not, enjoy your present. You are so damn lucky."

Chapter 7

Okay, once you sign this, I can give you your license back and you can head back to your campsite. Here's your map, your site ticket, hangtag and a trash bag for you," said the elderly woman at the campgrounds window, the pink stripe in her hair jiggling slightly, mimicking the palsy in her hands.

"Okay, thanks. Um, how will I know which one is mine and where to go?" asked Ruby, peering down the lane as it disappeared into a canopy of trees.

"Have you ever been here before?"

"No, I've never been to a campground before, and not with a trailer."

"Oh boy. We've got a newbie. Clem?" The pink stripe turned her head and hollered back over her shoulder. "Clem, we have a newbie. She's a cute young thing."

Presumably Clem walked up and craned his head out the window. They looked like a set of Siamese twins from a bad sit-com.

"You never been camping?" Clem appraised her Jeep as they stretched further out the window. "You got yourself one of them new little cat can trailers. Tiny little thing. Damned expensive, though. How come you got something so little when you could've had something bigger for the same price?" Clem rolled the toothpick in his mouth around thoughtfully.

"Clem, don't be rude. Can't you see she's alone? Probably better she got herself a little trailer."

"Helen, she's wearing a wedding ring. See there on the steering wheel?"

"Shhh. Clem. It ain't none of yer business. Now why don't you get the cart and lead her to her campsite. She is in C-21." Helen looked at Ruby. "Do you want some firewood? Clem can put that in the cart and take it to your site for you. That'd be seven dollars for the wood, a single bundle. If you want it that is." She looked at Ruby, expectantly.

"Sure, fire wood will be great."

"One bundle or two?"

"Two. Two would be great." Ruby paid for the wood and put the car into drive, waiting as Clem came out of the office building and jumped into his cart.

"The camp store is open until nine, so when you realize you need fire starter you should come get it before we close." Helen smiled gleefully at Ruby, then closed the sliding window with a bang.

Ruby followed Clem to the firewood station and waited patiently until he loaded two big bundles of wood into the back. Then he hopped on and drove through the canopy of trees

Clem twisted and turned his way through the various roads, Ruby following him, trying to pay attention to the signs. She wanted to be sure she could find her way out when the time came. The roads were very narrow, and it took a minute for her to realize that most of them were one way. They reached a sign that said, C-Loop. Clem turned right, and she followed him down the narrower land. There were a lot of campers in C-Loop, all backed into a campsite. Little wooden signs by the side of the driveway marked the campsite number. Each campsite had a tag attached indicating which nights the site was reserved.

Clem stopped in front of site twenty-one and pointed. She was supposed to back her trailer into that little drive? It was at an angle. It was between two trees. There was a ditch on each side of the driveway. Her hands started to sweat. She had practiced in parking lots, but they were wide open. The storage yard where she had parked it until she was ready to go provided a spot she could pull right into then pull straight out to leave. How the hell was she going to do this?

Clem got out of the golf cart and put his hands on his hips. He was waiting for her to back up. She heard voices and saw Clem look over his shoulder. He said something and then jerked his thumb over his shoulder, pointing at her. Ruby saw he was talking to a couple in the campsite directly across the road from hers. She watched as the couple each grabbed a chair and sat down to watch the show. Unbelievable, she thought. Un-freaking-believable.

Clem limped over to her.

"What's the problem? You do know how to back that little trailer up, don't you?"

"Sure, I do. It's just that there are those trees, and..." Ruby's voice trailed off.

"I'll help you. Just watch my hand signals."

Ruby put the Jeep in reverse and started to back up. She was immediately grateful for the new set of mirrors she had the dealer put on the Jeep. It was so much easier to see ... to see the tree, the damn tree, oh shit! She slammed on the brakes and put the Jeep into drive inching forward.

"Aren't you watching my hand signals?" Clem came up to the window. He noticed the beads of sweat on her forehead. "Hell, you ain't as close to that tree as you think. Now take it slow and you'll be fine. Straighten out your wheel and back up

25

slowly." Ruby turned the wheel. "No, this way." Clem reached into the Jeep and turned the wheel the other way. "Do you want to go into the damn ditch?" He checked the tires, looked at the trailer. Satisfied, he told her to try again.

This time Ruby inched back slowly, turning the wheel a little at a time, being careful not to over steer.

"That's it." Clem yelled. "Come on out and see how you did."

Ruby stepped out of the Jeep and was surprised to hear thunderous clapping. Not only did the couple across the road applaud her efforts but both sets of families on either side of her did, too. Even a toddler got in on the action. Ruby's face turned the color of her name, but she bowed gracefully to her audience.

"You'll do better next time," Clem said kindly. "We all start off having trouble. Hell, I saw a guy last week have the damnedest time trying to back in this very spot, and he had been camping for years. Claimed something was reflecting light in his eyes, or some other damned thing. Well, we'll see you up to the store when you come to buy your fire starter." With that Clem jumped into his golf cart and sped away.

Chapter 8

Ruby had the fire crackling merrily when Clem stopped back again in his golf cart. She grinned to herself, knowing he wondered how she managed to light all those big logs without stopping by his camp store. She had told Helen that she had never been to a campground before, nor had she ever camped in a trailer. That was true. What she didn't tell Helen was that she had spent many nights out in the woods. When she was in sixth grade, she had a small tent she found discarded on garbage day. She often walked home from school on the days people set their garbage out for pickup. This is where she scored some of her most prize possessions.

One spring day, she found a narrow little drawstring bundle on the curb. Curious, she picked it up and looked inside. Still not sure what it was, she hoisted it on her shoulder and carried it home. Her dad wasn't home from work yet, so she put on her play clothes and took the object outside to the backyard. She had learned early to always check the items she scavenged outside before she took them into the house. You never knew what kind of nasty stuff might be mixed in with treasure.

What she discovered was she was now the proud owner of

a small backpacking tent. The instructions for setting it up were printed on a tag connected to the bag. She studied the instructions, and it didn't take her too long to figure out how the tent went together. Once it was up, she crawled inside and marveled at her new private space. She couldn't wait to camp in it.

She wondered why it had been discarded. She couldn't find anything wrong with it. That weekend, when her daddy passed out drunk, she carted her tent out to the backyard and spent her first night under the stars. It was chilly in the evening, but she loved the sense of freedom, and the feeling of being in a womb.

There was hell to pay in the morning, because she'd slept late and didn't have her dad's breakfast on the table, but it was worth it. When she went to school the next week, she checked out of the library all the books she could find about camping in the woods. She immersed herself in the world of camping and read about how to start fires, the best places to pitch a tent, and wondrous adventures like thru-hiking the Appalachian Trail.

When she lay in her tent at night, her imagination took her on those hikes, exploring places with exotic sounding names like Springer Mountain, Clingman's Dome, Mt. Katahdin. Her ragged tent took her to college, where weekends found her escaping to the national forests, returning to her childhood methods of sidestepping the world when it closed in on her.

She avoided crowds, but occasionally camped with college friends. They shunned the established campgrounds because they cost money, and campers were under the watchful eye of the campground ranger. Instead, they preferred the sanctuary of the forest, where they could drink their beer in peace and unwind from the week.

When Ruby met George, she found someone who wasn't interested in camping but was interested in her. They went once or twice, but her little tent wasn't big enough for the two of them. He wined and dined her and turned her away from needing to escape to the woods. She became comfortable in his presence and recognized a good thing when she had it.

As the years passed, the wild yearning returned to her heart. The comfortable existence with George was steady, but she missed the night breeze in her tent and the call of the owl in the early hours before dawn.

Now, George, that steady, protective presence was gone. She could have all the adventure she wanted, but now she really didn't. She just wanted George back.

The snapping of the fire brought her back to her senses. She sniffed the air appreciatively, smelling the garlic in the roasting potatoes that were wrapped tightly in foil along with sliced polish sausages and onions. In the small Dutch oven next to the fire, garlic bubble bread was turning a golden brown. George would have loved this, she thought. Not the camping, but the garlic bread would have made him swoon. She wondered why she had never made it for him. The Dutch oven had sat in their basement unused for the last twenty-four years. "Oh George, how much I gave up for you, but how much you missed out on." She immediately felt guilty for the traitorous thought.

"That smells mighty good over here. I see you got your fire started just fine. Who helped you out with that?" asked Clem, as he meandered over to the fire, followed closely by Helen, who looked curiously at the campsite.

"Yeah, I got it started all by my little self," said Ruby, sarcastically.

"Now, Clem don't be mean. She looks like she is doing just fine. What a cute little Dutch oven. What's in it?"

"I made garlic bread to go with my foil packet," Ruby said, watching Clem inch closer.

"I have to say, that bread smells mighty fine. Mighty fine indeed."

"Well, thank you. It still has a while to cook yet. Can I help you with something?"

"No, no. We just closed the store, and we wanted to be sure our newbie camper was doing okay, but I get the feeling you may have been fibbing to us. You certainly aren't a newbie to campfire cooking." He looked at her accusingly, his eyes squinting.

"I said I have never camped in a campground like this or in a trailer, but I am not new to camping. This is a civilized version of what I am used to." Ruby remarked. "I need to learn how to better back up this thing," she gestured to the trailer, "and I will probably amuse the entire campground when it comes time to empty the sewage tanks, but I can hold my own primitive camping, thank you."

"Well, we will leave you be, then," said Helen, pulling on Clem's shirt sleeve. "COME ON, Clem, I have dinner in the crock-pot at our site. We have a nice pot roast with potatoes and carrots." Helen had a superior look, certain her pot roast had no competition in the camp cuisine department.

"Enjoy your dinner then," said Ruby. "Good night."

Helen and Clem got back in their golf cart and glided quietly away, heading back to their giant fifth wheel camper parked next to the camp office.

Ruby stretched back in her camp chair and gazed up at the stars. It had gotten quiet. Campfires dotted the evening, and voices were reduced to murmurs. Using the lid lifter, Ruby peeked at the garlic bread. It was golden brown and perfectly cooked. Quickly, she brushed some melted butter on the top and sprinkled the surface with grated Romano cheese and some parsley flakes. Her face had a satisfied smirk. It looked like a freaking magazine picture. It had been many, many years since she had made this recipe, but it seemed like she hadn't lost her touch.

She popped into her little camper and retrieved a paper

plate and some plastic ware. She would have to buy dishes for the teardrop, but she hadn't gotten that far yet. She slipped the foil packet on her plate and unfolded the seam. The smell of fragrant herbs, rosemary and thyme filled the air. The slices of polish sausage swelled against their casing, bursting with flavor, and the potatoes fell apart when her fork touched it. She added two garlic bread bubbles, then settled back to enjoy her first camp dinner in years.

Only, she had to enjoy it alone.

T he fire was out, and wispy clouds covered the moon low on the horizon. Ruby was getting chilled, so she figured it was time to spend her first night in the tiny camper. She had been dreading this moment and was putting it off as long as she could. George bought this for her. She had a sneaking suspicion George figured he would never spend a single night in it. This was the only big possession in her life she hadn't shared with George. Their house still had his essence wherever she looked. She couldn't bring herself to remove that Cleveland baseball hat from his side table, or that damn losing football stadium blanket from the back of his easy chair. His sedan still sat in the driveway, next to hers. Waiting for him. Everything was still waiting for him. Except the trailer. He wasn't in the trailer. His scent didn't linger there. She wouldn't find a stray sock behind a piece of furniture. She would sleep alone. Completely alone.

She opened the narrow door and entered the tiny trailer. On her right was a small counter that served as her kitchen. The counter held a stovetop that could be covered by a counter board, and a sink which also could be hidden in the same manner. A tiny oven and refrigerator were in the cabinets below. Above were small cabinets intended for storage, but there wasn't much room for even the essentials.

If she turned left, she was facing the back of the trailer. Next to the kitchen counter was a small cabinet that the trailer company extolled as a bathroom. Opening the door revealed a camper toilet and an amazingly tiny shower. If she took two steps forward from the kitchen, she could either sit at the tiny dinette or crawl in her queen-sized bed, depending upon how it was configured at the time. This engineering marvel covered the rear area of the trail, nesting under the sloping teardrop roof. The best feature was a sliding observation panel that allowed her to watch the stars at night. In the back of her mind, she worried that it would leak when it rained. She remembered hearing somewhere that skylights always leaked. Well, she would cross that bridge when she came to it.

The camper felt stuffy, so she opened all the little windows and cracked the roof vent. She flipped the switch for the fan and turned it to exhaust. She remembered reading in the manual it would be efficient in cooling the trailer if the trailer had been closed up.

Within minutes, the trailer was comfortably cool. She turned the fan to low and crawled into the little bed. She lay there. Alone. In silence. Alone. It was crazy. All those years as a kid, relishing the nights in the tent, alone, at peace. But this alone felt different. Where was that steady breathing that always ended in a light snore? Where was that hand that always reached over and cupped her breast? What the hell had happened to her life?

She sat up and looked around her. She was restless. Some people would feel claustrophobic in the tiny space, but she thought it was luxurious compared to her two-man back-packing tent she used to sleep in. This was a positive castle, but something wasn't quite right. It was too... sanitary. Too perfect. It wasn't lived in. She sighed. It would take time to make it feel like… hers. That was it. This was hers. Not hers and George's, but hers. She could make it however she wanted. She could be sloppy or neat. She could stick travel stickers all over the walls. That would make George crazy, she thought. She stopped herself. He wasn't here to get crazy. He. Wasn't. Here. He would never be here again.

She lay back down and looked at the stars through the skylight, tears running sideways down her cheeks and into her ears. George would have known she would love this. He knew she would love the teardrop. He even knew she would love the small size of the trailer, and that it would be perfect for her. She just had to get used to the idea. No, she would never get used to the idea.

Chapter 9

S taring into space again?" Laney Brunner, Ruby's boss and best friend, stopped in front of Ruby's desk. Ruby looked up sheepishly and grinned.

"Yeah, you caught me. I will admit I am having a hard time concentrating on laundry techniques to keep your clothes looking fresh." She sat up straighter and stretched her spine.

"Come on, let's go get a cup of coffee." Laney suggested.

"No, but thanks. I need to finish this, and I have a couple more articles in my in-box."

"I am well aware of that. This is not a request. This is more like an order... from your boss." Laney looked steadily down at Ruby and watched as Ruby's face colored.

"I'm sorry. I didn't realize. I mean..." Ruby stammered.

"Cut it out. It's the only way I can get your attention lately. I have to pull the boss card. Come on, my treat. Besides, there is something I want to talk to you about." With that, the petite, extremely well put together Laney turned, knowing full-well Ruby would follow. Ruby cursed her friend's confidence.

The day was warm, and the sun was a welcome change after the last week of rains that had plagued the region. Late

Spring in Northeast Ohio was a crap shoot. It could rain, snow, sleet, and then scorch you, all within a twenty-four-hour period. Today, the world was loving the change of luck with the weather.

They both grabbed a mocha at their favorite indy coffee shop and snagged a table near a flowering crab tree. It was a perfect place, and normally Ruby would have been in heaven, but she was distracted and out of sorts. Laney watched her friend squirm, uncomfortable with the moment.

"Ruby, it's only been a month since George passed. I don't expect you to be your old self, but I'm worried about you." Laney reached across the table and covered Ruby's hand. Ruby squirmed at the intimacy. She was never one to hug or touch, even her best friend. Laney slowly drew her hand back but held Ruby with her gaze. "You have every right to be sad, but you haven't allowed yourself to grieve. You took two days off when George died. His funeral was on the weekend, and then you came back to work. You have been driving yourself hard. My guess is you do it so you don't have to think about it, but at night, you have yourself locked in your house. You have refused to have dinner with me. I know Barb called you last week, but you turned her down, and Pat said you avoided her in the cafeteria. That's not like you. Come on honey. Talk to me."

"I'm sorry." Ruby ducked her head and sipped her mocha. Stalling. Laney waited patiently. The first person to talk loses. Ruby sighed. "It's just so weird with George gone. I still can't wrap my head around it. I see him everywhere. I hear his voice. I catch a whiff of his aftershave, and he is with me. I don't know what to do, and I don't know how to move on. The only place he isn't is in that little trailer he bought me."

"Well, that's what I wanted to talk with you about. You camped in that sardine tin once, didn't you?"

Ruby nodded her head, and a wistful smile tweaked the corner of her mouth. The movement wasn't lost on Laney.

"I want you to take some time off from the office." Laney held up her hand as Ruby started to protest. "No, I am serious. Only it's not a vacation. I actually have a job for you." Laney waited, looking for a spark of interest in Ruby's eyes. It wasn't there. Laney plunged on.

"One of the magazines you edit for contacted me. They like your editing style, and they asked if you were interested in doing some writing. Have you ever thought of that?" Laney could see the gears start to turn in Ruby's head.

"What kind of writing?" asked Ruby, suspicious.

"It's a travel magazine. They are looking for articles written by people on the road, the up close and personal aspect of the great outdoors stuff. Honestly, that stuff is beyond me. If there isn't a Starbucks and a hot tub, it isn't a vacation. But what do you think?"

"I think you think I'm stupid," said Ruby, bluntly.

Laney was taken aback. Ruby usually wasn't so abrupt, but then, Ruby was smart. She should have known.

"I don't think you're stupid. I think this would be good for you. Whatever. Your first assignment is to write an article about living in that cat can you call a trailer in a national forest. I have the details back at my desk. They want the article in two weeks, so I expect that you will have that done. HR knows you will be out of the office for the next two weeks, and Emma knows not to assign you any more editing jobs. Let me know if you need anything, and I will see what I can do." Laney delivered the last statement with an air of efficiency that reminded Ruby that not only was Laney her friend, but she also signed her checks.

Chapter 10

R uby consulted the map. She was looking for the forest
road that led to a primitive campground about five
miles in. Kylie assured her that her little teardrop had off-road
capabilities. Kylie reminded her that Ruby's husband had
bought her the best of the best. Well, here it goes, Ruby
thought.

She turned on the small road and began the descent into
the valley. It wasn't as rough as she was afraid it would be.
The road rambled through the forest, then through a meadow.
She passed a pair of white-tail deer delicately nibbling on some
spring flowers that were blooming. They watched her mildly as
she drove slowly by. Ruby felt the tension in her shoulders
begin to melt away.

It had been a difficult trip here. She ran into a couple of
driving rain storms that set her on edge. She wasn't used to
towing a trailer and not being able to see through the rain
made her even more uptight. She second guessed herself
repeatedly while she packed. She wasn't sure what all she
would need for the trip, and the teardrop didn't hold a lot. She
figured she wasn't going to be socializing, but she didn't want

to sit around in stinky clothes. On the way, she had to stop at an outfitters store and buy a solar charger with a battery pack to keep her cell phone and computer charged. She had her doubts about the electrical set-up in the camper, but Kylie promised her that the camper batteries would last a long time.

Ruby had trust issues.

She wanted back up. She priced a small generator, but she wasn't fond of the noise generators made, and the one she looked at was too heavy and took up too much space. No, she was going to go minimalist. On an impulse, she bought a solar shower. Granted, she had a shower in the camper, but she liked the idea of not using her energy for that. She had gotten a later start than she had wanted, and she felt like the trip was starting off rocky. That made her even more stressed.

Despite her tension, the deeper she pulled into the forest, the more relaxed she became. She came upon a wooden sign that indicated the camping area was off to the right. Ah, this was so much better than the amusement park camping at the last place. There was no one else here. The forest was quiet, and the campsites were situated well away from each other. In fact, there were trees and low vegetation between each camp area, so the sites felt extremely secluded. Ruby was going to like this.

According to the national forest brochure, she was supposed to select her site and then fill out the form at the little wooden kiosk where she turned into the campground. She parked her Jeep and checked out each site. She selected the furthest one on the turnaround and expertly backed her trailer into the spot. She was a lot better at it without an audience. She grabbed a pen from the center console and pulled some money from her wallet. Locking the Jeep out of habit, she walked up the lane, heading for the kiosk to settle up with the U. S. Government.

She completed the form, counted out the bills, and sealed

everything in the envelope provided. Then she looked around trying to decide just what to do with the payment. She spotted a large pipe sticking out of the ground. The side had a slot cut into it and a small sign instructed campers to drop their payments in the pipe. Ruby obliged and started back to her camper.

A movement in the bushes on her right startled her. *Pay attention.* She heard George's voice in her head. It took her breath away. *You are here all alone. You are a woman with no protection. Pay attention.* She shook her head, not allowing herself to get spooked. Yes, George had been her protector, but he wasn't around when she was a kid, and she took pretty good care of herself then. She could do so again now. The bushes rustled again. She quickened her step, then began to whistle a low tune, kind of quiet, soothing. The forest quieted. She laughed at herself. Probably a damn squirrel or chipmunk. *I would be lucky to see any interesting wildlife.*

She reached her camper and finished her camp set up. She set up her side awning and unfolded her chair. She had purchased a tiny folding side table, so she set that up and plopped a citronella candle in a metal decorative lantern down on top. There, she thought. All the comforts of home.

R uby squeezed the teardrop-shaped tinfoil package that she had nestled between some rocks over hot coals. The contents gave easily to her squeeze. Her dinner was almost ready, and not a minute too soon. The first fat raindrops were starting to fall. Using a pair of leather gloves, she carefully plucked the package out of the fire and carried it to the small side table under her awning. She went back and retrieved the cast iron skillet holding the golden grilled cheese sandwich. She sighed, content. This was one of her favorite camping meals. Her best friend in college, Tracy, taught her how to make French onion soup over coals. It was one of the last things Tracy ever taught her. Tracy had found the man of her dreams, and they got married, barefoot on a rock. Then the whole party dined on pizza from a strange pizza place near the Red River Gorge. It was like a flashback to the sixties, hippies and all. After that, Tracy and her man headed west, and Ruby lost touch. She wondered if she could somehow get in contact with her again.

Ruby lifted the foil packet and placed it in a deep soup bowl. She carefully untwisted the pointy tail that served as a handle. The aroma of rich beef broth and savory onions filled the air. Ruby quickly dumped a handful of croutons in the packet and lay two slices of Swiss cheese over the contents, then twisted the foil again over the top. While she waited, she took a sip of the mojito she had crafted for herself in anticipation of dinner. The refreshing minty lime drink quenched her thirst, and she stretched out her legs and leaned back in her chair, enjoying relaxing before her meal. She loved the feeling of not being rushed. After a few minutes, she peeked inside the foil. The cheese had melted over the croutons and the soup was ready. Dinner was on.

Ruby ate heartily. Her appetite seemed like it was finally returning. She had lost a good ten pounds since George's funeral. She was never really heavy, and the weight loss left her looking a little gaunt. As she ate her food, she felt ravenous. Yep, the appetite was definitely returning.

She was finishing her last bite of the soft center of her grilled cheese and was ready to start devouring the crusts she had saved for last when she heard a soft cry. Startled, she looked around.

Creeping on its belly from behind her chair was a muddy matted animal, its bright eyes peering below a set of scruffy eyebrows.

"Hello, dog," said Ruby. "You are a pathetic looking mess." The dog twitched just the end of its tail and crept closer, its tongue nervously licking its lips, its nose twitching.

Ruby took a bite of the crust. The dog followed every move.

"Are you hungry?" The dog whimpered and shivered in anticipation.

"I'll have you know this is my favorite part of a grilled cheese sandwich." The dog bowed his head at her words and looked dejected. Ruby laughed and tossed what was left of the first crust over to the dog. He snatched it and wolfed it down. Then he politely wagged his tail and lifted his right paw. He looked pointedly at the other crust laying on her plate.

"Seriously? You want the other crust?"

"Woof," the dog vocalized, softly.

"What the hell. I still have some mojito, so I guess you can have this." She threw the remaining crust to the dog, and he snatched it and ran into the woods.

"You're welcome, you ungrateful cur," she called after the beast.

She finished sipping her drink as the rain continued to fall. Her fire was out, no longer sizzling and steaming in the raindrops.

The next morning, Ruby peered out the little window in the door of her camper. The day was gray and drizzling. She snuggled back into bed with a book and read the morning away. She could get used to this. A few hours later the rain was still coming down. She made her bed and set up her table so she could use the dinette during the day. She used her little kitchen for the first time and made herself some eggs. She poured a steaming mug of coffee and sat at the table writing up her notes regarding her first night in the forest.

Satisfied with her progress, she cleaned up her mess in the kitchen enjoying the clever arrangement of the tiny space.

Once everything was put away to her liking, she dug in the storage compartment under the dinette cushions and pulled out her waterproof hiking boots. She was going to slog through the woods despite the miserable weather.

Ruby emerged from the trailer in a pair of quick dry hiking shorts and a button-down shirt. She carried a small backpack with an extra bottle of water and her raincoat stuffed inside. It had finally stopped raining, but it would probably start again at any minute. As she unlocked her Jeep to retrieve her hiking sticks, she heard a muffled scraping noise behind her. She turned in time to see the dog from last night wiggle his way from under the camper. He shook his dirty matted coat and looked up at her as if to say where are we going?

"I thought about hiking to Cascade Falls." Ruby addressed the dog. He wagged his tail in approval. "It's a three-mile hike one way. Are you up for a quick six miles?" He woofed at her and wagged his tail again.

She reached to pet him, but he shied away. She held her hand still, waiting for him to come to her. One step, a half. A tiny tongue reached out, just the tip of it, touching her hand. Then he jumped back. He wagged his tail in apology.

Ruby didn't move but murmured to him in a soft voice. Once again, he stepped forward. She touched his ear with her fingertips. He held still, stiff. She scratched, carefully. Dirt collected under her nails. He stepped one more step forward. She petted his neck with her whole hand. He quivered under her touch. His hair was filthy, matted, and covered with burs.

"You need a bath, buddy. Hang on." She stood up slowly and disappeared into the camper. She came out stuffing a small bottle into her backpack along with a large supply of granola bars.

"Ya want breakfast?" She broke up one of the granola bars into small pieces and tossed him one. He wolfed it down. She crouched down again and held a piece out to him. This time he walked forward with confidence, and with gentle manners, he took the food from her fingers properly. Ruby scratched his grizzled head, then wiped her dirty hands on her pants.

"We really have to give you a bath. Come on buddy, let's go hiking."

Chapter 11

The trail was muddy, but as it climbed into the highlands, the drainage was better. The rain had cleared, and the sun was peeking out from behind the clouds. Ruby enjoyed the trek through the woods with the little dog. Sometimes he led the way, his nose to the ground, sniffing his way, other times, he lagged behind, exploring behind bushes, or sticking his nose in holes he found in the ground. He always came bounding up to her when he was finished, tilting his face to hers, his bright, intelligent eyes searching hers.

After three miles and no water fall, Ruby consulted her trail map. It wasn't very detailed, just a free, printed forest map with a squiggly line representing the trail. Maybe it was just a little further.

"Where is that promised water fall, huh, buddy?" The dog wagged his tail, and moved ahead, strutting confidently down the trail. Ruby shrugged and followed. The trail turned around the back of a small bluff and then descended into a valley. Within minutes, Ruby could hear rushing water. Another five minutes of hiking and they were there.

Wagging his tail, the dog put his front feet into the rushing stream water and lapped happily. Ruby found a large rock, and she perched herself on it in the sunshine. She pulled out her water bottle and had a drink herself. As she went to replace the water bottle, a small plastic bottle fell out of her pack. Well, here goes, she thought to herself.

"Hey buddy, ya wanna bath? No offense, but you're really, really dirty, and you kinda smell."

The dog looked at her curiously, then put his head down for another drink. Ruby approached him slowly. The dog glanced at her warily. He knew something was up.

"So, I am just going to get you wet, then use this biodegradable shampoo on you. It will feel wonderful, I promise."

The dog licked his lips nervously but didn't move from the stream.

"That's really not a good spot. The water is running fast, and I bet it is cold. Come over here. There is a small, shallow pool. I bet the sun has warmed it up. Come on, buddy. Come here."

The dog hesitated, then came forward slowly. Ruby crouched down beside the pool and waited patiently. She wouldn't look at him. She put her fingers in the water and swirled them lazily. The sun had made the little pool a lot warmer than the main part of the stream.

She felt a presence next to her, so she looked to her left. The little dog sat next to her, watching her fingers play in the water.

"Go on buddy. Go on in the water." She urged him with her voice. He stood up and waded in the water to her fingers, then licked them.

Ruby pet him and carefully splashed handfuls of water over his back. The dog slowly relaxed and allowed Ruby to give him a makeshift bath.

When she got to his neck, he whimpered a little. The silver

buckle on the leather collar was wrapped tightly in his fur. She had inadvertently pulled his hair and pinched his skin when she lathered around the collar. She tried to take it off, but it was knotted tightly in the short hairs of his neck. She held the collar still with one hand and shampooed around it with the other. She would use her knife back at the camper and cut the collar free of the fur when she got back.

By the time she was rinsing the shampoo out of the dogs fur he was closing his eyes and quivering with delight. It was obvious he was enjoying the feeling of her hands massaging his body. When she was done, he showered her hands with kisses. She shared another granola bar with him and then sat back on the warm rock to watch the water cascade down the falls.

They both may have dozed off in the sun, but something had awakened Ruby. The sun had hidden behind another cloud, and a chill wind started to blow. Ruby grabbed her backpack and picked up her granola wrappers.

"I think we'd better head back, buddy. I think it's going to rain again." The dog opened one eye and sighed. He had been enjoying his snooze next to her on the warm rock. He got up and stretched his hind legs, one at a time. Then he bowed forward, stretching his back. He looked up at her and shook himself, ears flapping, tail twisting.

"Are you finished? Come on, let's get going." They set off for the trailer.

They reached the campsite just as big drops of rain pelted the leafy canopy. Ruby stowed her backpack in the trailer and came out with a small pair of nail scissors.

"This will work better than a knife." Ruby sat in her chair under the awning and patted her thighs with her hands. "Come on up, buddy."

The dog wagged the tip of his tail, tentatively, hesitated, then jumped gracefully into her lap. She stroked the now mostly clean coat. The fur was no longer caked with dirt, but it still looked like it needed a good brushing. She had a feeling, however, that no matter how much she brushed it, the coat would always have a wiry, unkempt look. She carefully took the scissors and snipped the hair wound around the buckle of the collar. There were a couple of burrs thrown in the mix that were making it even harder to cut the collar free. Ruby was afraid of snipping the dog's skin. It was hard to tell where the matted fur ended and skin began. The dog stretched out his neck and closed his eyes, holding himself stiffly. It seemed as if he were trying to help her.

When the collar was cut free, the dog jumped off Ruby's lap and shook his body gleefully. Then he ran around in circles and threw himself down, sliding sideways on a patch of grass, first with his muzzle, then with the side of his neck. He finished by rolling on his back and wiggling back and forth, all four paws waving in the air. After a few minutes of pure bliss, he stood up, shook, and walked in a dignified manner back to Ruby, as if none of that had happened. She laughed and scratched behind his ears, his coat wet again from the recent rain and the wet grass. He closed his eyes, leaned into her hand and groaned.

Ruby reached down and picked up the leather collar that had fallen to the ground. She could tell it was high-quality leather, but it was beyond dirty. She filled a plastic container with warm, soapy water and put the collar in to soak for a few minutes. She knew that wasn't the way to treat leather, but she figured it had seen worse. The dog sniffed the container and licked his lips.

"You poor thing. I'll bet you're thirsty and probably hungry, too. Where do you belong, and who is your master? Huh, buddy?" The dog stared at her with his bright eyes. "And what's your name? I keep calling you buddy, but it obviously isn't what you've been called all your life." The dog sneezed and looked at the container again.

"Hang on. Once the collar is done soaking, I'll wash it out and give you fresh water. You won't die waiting." He licked his lips again and looked at her half-full water bottle. Then he barked.

"You want to drink out of my water bottle? Seriously?" The dog came closer, looking at the water bottle and wagging his tail.

"I'm losing my mind," complained Ruby. "God only knows where your mouth has been or what parts you have been licking." She swore the dog grinned at her.

Ruby opened the cap and tipped it carefully. The dog turned his head and wrapped his tongue around the small stream of water pouring out of the bottle. Ruby lifted the bottle higher, keeping the lip of the bottle away from the dubiously clean dog tongue, and the dog lapped, satisfied. He sat back on his haunches when he was done and smiled a doggy smile with his mouth open, his lips stretched wide and a happy tongue cleaning the water droplets off his muzzle.

"You're a pretty smart dog. I'm sure your name isn't Spot."

The dog stared at her. "How about Sandy? Leo? Mortimer?" The dog sneezed in disgust. "I guess I'll just keep on calling you Buddy."

Ruby reached into the container and held the collar submerged while she scrubbed it with her fingers. It took work, but soon the leather felt smooth under her fingers, except for an area which felt like there might be some tooling. She pulled out the collar and wiped it off with some paper towels. Sure enough, the collar was embossed. She lay the collar flat, so she could see the entire design.

George.

Ruby's heart stopped.

George.

She looked at the dog. He was staring at her, steadily.

George.

She looked at the collar. Now her heart was pounding hard, slamming against her chest.

George.

The world tilted. The dog whimpered.

George.

Chapter 12

The next thing Ruby knew, the dog was in her lap, furiously washing her face with his tongue. When her eyes fluttered open, her jaw dropped, and a wet, sloppy dog tongue landed in her mouth.

"Oh, that's just too much. First, you have my dead husband's name, and now you're jamming your tongue down my throat. Get off me." George jumped down, his tail between his legs, looking dejected.

Ruby stared ahead, refusing to look at the dog. He whimpered. Ruby's jaw worked. She wouldn't look down. They were at an impasse.

The crunching of tires on gravel made Ruby turn her attention from staring off into space to looking for the source of the noise. Next to her, on the ground, George growled. A ranger truck stopped in front of her campsite.

"Good evening," said the Forest Service Ranger as he stepped out of the truck. He was a tall, solidly built man with a friendly smile and deep brown eyes.

"Good evening," responded Ruby. George responded with a hearty growl.

"Is everything okay, ma'am," said the ranger, picking up on the tension in the air.

Ruby thought about saying, sure, everything is just fine, but this stray dog who won't leave me alone has the same name as my husband who died last month, so yeah, everything is just dandy. Instead, she pulled herself together.

"Yeah, everything is fine. What can I do for you?"

"I was just making my rounds, and I saw that someone had paid for a campsite back here. This is one of our more secluded sites, so I thought I would come on back and check things out. You must be Ruby?" He saw her startled look, and he hurried to reassure her. "It says so on your campsite registration."

Ruby laughed, feeling foolish, and her face colored slightly.

"Of course," she said. "I am off my game, obviously."

"No worries." The ranger looked down at the dog at her feet. "What's your dog's name?"

"That is not my dog," she said, stifling a giggle, remembering the line from an old 70s movie.

The ranger's lips quirked up in a smirk. He's pretty good looking, thought Ruby, unexpectedly. Her gut twisted, and her heart hurt.

"Funny, but the dog needs to be kept on a leash. Since there is no one around, I'm not going to give you a hard time, but if another camper comes, please be sure to tie him up or keep him leashed. Okay?"

"No, seriously, George isn't my dog. He's a stray."

"George? You know the dog's name, but he's not yours? He's a stray?" The ranger looked at her amused. Ruby got flustered under his steady stare.

"His collar. It says George. He has been hanging around here since yesterday. He was dirty and matted. I gave him a bath and cut the collar out of his fur where it was tangled.

The collar says George. So, I figured his name is George, and he is not my dog."

"It looks like he thinks he's your dog." The ranger gestured at George. Ruby looked down to see George facing the ranger with his left lip lifted in a tiny snarl, a warning that the dog didn't like the ranger's attitude.

"George, stop that!" Ruby admonished. George lowered his lip and sat but remained alert and stared at the ranger.

"Yep, that's your dog." Again, the ranger smiled his dazzling smile.

"Well, the dog that is not my dog, does not have any food. He has to belong to someone around here. Have you ever seen him before?" Ruby asked feeling frustrated.

"I may have seen him around." The ranger was strangely evasive. "We have a lot of people coming through here every week. He could have come from anywhere. So, you're saying this little guy hasn't had anything to eat for at least the last two days?"

"He had the crusts from my grilled cheese sandwich and a granola bar. That's it, as far as I know. He really has to be hungry." When Ruby said the word, hungry, George's ears perked up, and he barked. Ruby and the ranger looked at George in surprise.

"Are you hungry, George?" asked Ruby. George wagged his tail and barked sharply.

"Do you want something to eat?" asked the ranger. George looked at him with disgust, but then sat in front of him and lifted his right paw.

"I think we're going to have to find this dog some food. You guys want to come for a ride? I'll take you over the ridge to the country market. They have dog food. Then we can get your dog food and maybe a leash. What do you say?"

"I don't even know you, and this is not my dog."

"My name is Adam, so now you know me. Are you and your dog coming or not?"

Ruby looked at him, exasperated, then laughed.

"Okay, let me close up the trailer and get my wallet." Ruby disappeared into the trailer. George stood guard at the door, blocking the ranger's way. He stared into Adam's eyes until Ruby came back with her wallet and cell phone. "Why are you doing this?" asked Ruby, suspiciously.

"I think it's a crime you came here without any food for your dog, and I wouldn't be able to sleep tonight knowing there is a bad dog owner in my campground and I did nothing to help the poor beast." Ruby straightened her shoulders and set her jaw. The nerve of this guy. Adam laughed again. "Lighten up. I was joking. I figure if you can be kind enough to clean up a stray dog and help him with a collar that is stuck in his fur, then I can help make sure the little guy has something to eat. What do you say? You want to partner up and help this pup or no? Besides, you can't have your dog in my park without a leash."

"IT IS NOT MY DOG!" Ruby shouted, laughing as she climbed into the ranger's truck. George jumped in after her and settled on her lap, his nose poking out the open window, sniffing the breeze. Despite the fact that he wasn't all that fond of the ranger, he looked really happy to get to go for a ride.

Adam grinned at Ruby, put the truck in drive, and they headed down the lane to get her dog food and a leash.

"Rich, how are you?" Adam was smiling into the phone. Ruby could hear the response on the other end.

"I'm just dandy, Adam. You want something, so just come out and say it."

"That hurts, Rich, hurts to the core." Adam laughed as he said it, deep and warm.

"Let's look at this logically. You never call me at work, it's not wing night at The Barn, and your sister and I are still dating and happy, so what do you want?" The disembodied voice sounded amused, not irritated.

"Okay, you know me well, but wings tomorrow night? You bring Val, and I will bring Ruby. Sound good?" Ruby stared at him, her jaw hanging loose in disbelief. Adam winked at her.

"Ruby, who's Ruby? Wait, you still want something. This is a ploy."

"I have a situation. Ruby is a lady who is camping down at the bottoms. She has a dog that needs looked at."

"Is it an emergency? If so, you should take it to the clinic in Burton."

"No, it's not an emergency. She just picked up a stray, and I think he should be looked at. She was kind enough to give this poor guy a home, but a vet visit is in order. Do you have a minute?"

"Sure, anything for you. Besides, one good turn deserves another. Plus, I am curious how you got this lady to go out with you for wings."

Adam said goodbye and put his hand up to stop Ruby who was already sputtering.

"Now before you get yourself all wound up, let me just say I know how to get what I want, when I want it. I want Rich to take a look at George. Check. I want my sister to get off my back. You are going to help me out by having dinner with me tomorrow. Wings. Check. George will get the attention he needs from the vet, I will get the attention off of me from my sister, and you will get yourself a nice dog. It's a win win." Adam grinned at her, cocky and sure of himself.

"Not my dog," Ruby returned.

"Bet," Adam responded.

Ruby turned and looked out the window for the remainder of the trip. George spent the drive staring steadily at Adam, his right lip curled slightly.

Adam stopped in front of a low brick building with an attractive sign announcing that this was a veterinarian's office. Ruby slid out of the truck when Adam opened the door for her, and she picked George up and carried him into the building. An attractive man in a white lab coat stood behind the counter. He looked up as they came in and grinned at them.

"You must be Ruby, who rescued the stray, and who Adam has convinced to have wings with him tomorrow night. Is my assessment correct?"

Ruby laughed and replied. "You have part of that right, and you must be Rich."

"That I am. Hey, Adam." Adam nodded at him. George growled deep in his throat.

"Hello, fella." Rich reached out his hand and gently stroked George's ears. George stiffened, but tolerated it. "Hey, lighten up, dog. Don't look a gift vet in the mouth."

Rich motioned for them to follow him into an exam room. He looked over the dog, checking his ears, nose, eyes, and felt all of his limbs, back and abdomen. He picked up the dog's paws and looked at the bottom of his feet.

"Well, what you have is a Border Terrier mix, who I would guess is about three or four years old. He looks like he is in reasonable shape, but underweight. I will give him a round of vaccinations and some worm medicine. Make sure you mix a packet with his food once a day until it is gone. Other than that, feed him a good quality dog food, and he should fill out nicely."

"Wait, you don't understand. This is not my dog. He just stopped by my camper. I don't need a dog. I don't want a dog. I don't have time for a dog."

Adam and Rich watched her quietly, waiting for her to finish. George watched her, too. Rich lifted George's front right paw and showed Ruby the bottom.

"Look at this paw. This dog has been on the road for a long time. His paws are worn and sore. I think he was hoping your camper was his last stop. What do you think?"

Last stop. The words echoed in her head. Her husband's last words to her. I think this is my last stop. Last stop. George.

A tear slipped down Ruby's cheek. Adam and Rich looked at each other, startled.

"Wait," Adam said, "I didn't mean to push you into this."

George stepped across the table and stopped in front of Ruby. He reared onto his hind legs and put a front paw on each of her shoulders. He looked deeply into her sad eyes and carefully licked the tear from her cheek. She slipped her arms around the little dog and drew him close.

"George, this is your last stop. You're home. You're back with me."

Chapter 13

I'll start a fire. Will you need help with the food?" Adam asked as he crouched down at the fire ring and lay what would be a cooking fire.

"No, just get me a good bed of coals going. Do you want a mojito?" asked Ruby.

"What, like a mojito malt beverage or something in a bottle?"

"No, that would be disgusting. I mean an honest to goodness, Cuban inspired mojito with muddled mint leaves and lime. If you would rather have something from a bottle, I could probably run to the nearest store," Ruby yelled back sarcastically.

Adam popped his head into the trailer, looking around curiously. Ruby already had the steaks laid out and rubbed with fresh crushed garlic. She was oiling the potatoes and sprinkling them with coarse salt.

"Is the fire going?" she asked. Adam nodded. "Good, then wrap foil around these potatoes so we can bury them in the coals when they are ready." Adam squeezed next to her in the tiny kitchen, bumping elbows with her as he pulled out a length of foil.

"Sorry," he said, self-consciously. She looked at him sideways, enjoying his discomfort. She filled her little sink with water, covering the two ears of corn, soaking the husks. Adam brandished the foil-wrapped potatoes, showing off his skill.

"Nice," said Ruby. "In the fridge, you will find a bag of washed mint and a lime. Can you grab those for me while I mix up the butter? She softened butter in the microwave, then stirred in some chili powder while he rummaged in her mini-fridge.

"What's the problem?" she asked.

"Um, which is the mint?" Adam held up two bags of green leaves.

"Smell them, and you tell me." Ruby waited, rolling her eyes a little. Adam took a sniff. "Okay, I think this is mint, but what is the other?"

"The other is cilantro, and we need that too, unless you don't like it."

"No, cilantro is good."

Ruby cut a lime in half and squeezed a little into the butter mixture, then she added a handful of cilantro and stirred it all up.

"What is the butter for?" Adam asked.

"For the corn. We'll pull the husks back, put a little butter on the corn and bring the husks back over. We'll roast the corn in the wet husks. When they're done, we can use the rest of the butter on them. Does that sound okay?"

"Um, yeah, it sounds great. What else can I do?"

"You can see if those coals are ready, then bury the potatoes in them. They will take about an hour. We'll throw the steaks and the corn over the coals when the potatoes are done."

Adam went out with the potatoes, and Ruby set about

making two large mojitos. When she came outside, she spotted Adam laying a sweatshirt on the ground and patting it, encouraging George to lie on it. George looked cranky. George refused to comply.

Ruby laughed. "I don't think he likes you."

"After everything I did for him, you think he would."

"Here," Ruby handed Adam the drink. "That's sweet that you gave him your sweatshirt for a bed."

"Well, it's not my sweatshirt." Adam admitted. "It was left on a bench by the visitor center. No one claimed it for a couple of days, so it went in my truck. You never know when you will need a dog bed."

Adam sat down with his drink and stretched out his legs toward the fire.

"Hey, where did that chair come from?" Ruby asked.

"I always keep one in my truck. I need it when I can coerce a camper to share their dinner with me. I was an Eagle Scout. I am always prepared."

"Ah. Okay, Eagle Scout. Do you have a mess kit because I wasn't planning on guests? I travel light in my little camper."

"Believe it or not, I do." Adam started to get up when Ruby waved him back down.

"I was kidding. Notice you're drinking out of a glass, as am I?"

Ruby raised her glass and took a sip. Pure bliss reflected in her face. Adam took a tentative taste. Then he had another.

"Wow. You know how to make a mojito. This is amazing. Thank you." Ruby nodded. She grabbed the sweatshirt and drug it next to her chair, calling George to come over. He got up stiffly from where he was laying under the trailer.

"What's wrong with him? Why is he walking funny?" she asked.

"Poor George got a lot of shots today. He will be a little sore for a day or two."

The dog looked at the sweatshirt, then sniffed it. He stepped on it, turned three times, and laid down with a sigh. Within minutes he was snoring.

Ruby stared at the fire, relaxing with her mojito. She was trying to figure out just how she'd gotten here with a dog that was now apparently hers and a ranger sitting next to her expecting dinner in the next hour.

"What are you thinking?" Adam asked, tilting his head and looking at her.

"Just wondering why you're here?" Ruby looked at him, defiantly.

"I'm curious. I want to know your story. You obviously have one."

"What makes you think that?" Ruby took another sip of her mojito. Damn, it was good.

"Well, you're alone, but you're wearing a wedding ring. This camper is brand spanking new and so is all of your gear, but you know your way around a campsite. The camper can fit two people who really love each other, or at least get along well, but again, you are alone. The camper is outfitted for one. I had to get my own chair. I would have guessed divorce, but you don't seem bitter. You are sad though. It shows." Adam finished then waited quietly.

"Hmmm," is all Ruby said. They sat and sipped their drinks in silence. Adam leaned forward and checked the potatoes. They were still under cooked.

Ruby shifted in her chair and looked at him.

"So, what's your story? You want me to go with you to get wings tomorrow night to get your sister off your back. Why is she on your back?"

"Okay," said Adam. "I'll go first. I don't have a girlfriend. My sister is afraid I might be gay. She wants nieces and nephews someday."

"Why the hell would she think you're gay? You have that whole he-man park ranger thing going."

"Because I don't date girls." He waited for her response.

"Oh, I'm sorry. I didn't mean. Of course, gay guys can be park rangers. Oh shit." Ruby's face colored, and she took a big swallow of her drink.

Adam's eyes twinkled in amusement. He was enjoying her discomfort.

"I didn't say I was gay. I said I didn't date girls. At least not now. So, you will think I'm a jerk, but we don't know each other, and you will go on your way, never to be seen again, so I might as well tell you. I dated a girl in college. No wait, I fell in love with a girl in college. She was my everything. I would have given up the world for her. I almost did." He stopped to take a sip and stare into the fire. Ruby waited patiently.

"Well, she dumped me. She used me to buy her things, then she ran off with a guy who graduated med school. Doctors make a hell of a lot more money than rangers do."

"Bitch," said Ruby, companionably. Adam smiled in appreciation.

"So, I am not interested in a relationship. I don't want the hassle or the effort. I want to live life on my terms, and I want to do the things that interest me. I want to be selfish."

"Which is?" Ruby asked mildly, looking forlornly in her empty glass.

"I really don't know." Adam laughed. "But at least I don't have to explain it to a girlfriend. I will admit, I like companionship. I want female companionship with no strings attached." He looked at her sideways. "So, do you think I'm a jerk?"

"Nope. I think you're hurt, and I think you have a right to be. I also think that if you think we are going to hook up, no strings attached, you have another thing coming. Drink your drink, and I'll get the steaks and corn ready for the grill. Are those coals hot enough?"

Adam got the bed of coals ready under the grate, and Ruby came out with the food. She added some coarse salt and freshly cracked pepper to the steaks and threw them on the grill. She placed the corn next to them.

"Watch those while I get plates and silverware."

She emerged from the camper with a plastic table cloth and place settings. Adam set the table while Ruby disappeared into the camper again.

"Hey, can you flip those steaks?" she called from inside. "I like mine medium rare." She emerged with two fresh mojitos just as Adam was pulling the steaks off the grill. Ruby plopped a hunk of butter whipped with thyme on top of each steak, and Adam watched appreciatively as the butter melted into the grilled meat. Ruby tore the husks off the corn and buttered them generously with the cilantro lime butter. Adam removed the potatoes from the foil and put one on each plate. They looked at each other and grinned. Adam's stomach growled.

"What are you waiting for? You want this stuff to get cold?" scolded Ruby.

They dug into the food while George slept soundly on his sweatshirt.

Chapter 14

R uby lay in her bed, staring at her skylight and contemplating the stars twinkling merrily in the sky. But she didn't feel merry. She felt sad and guilty, and slightly woozy from the three mojitos she had downed that night.

After dinner, she and Adam sat around the fire enjoying the evening. They shared small talk, Ruby avoiding her marital situation. She didn't want to talk about George and his death. Explaining it to a stranger made it so final. Despite the fact that she had to do it over and over again when taking care of their financial affairs, presenting his death certificate as proof she wasn't just absconding with his cash, she still wasn't used to it. She hadn't yet called herself a widower, and she wasn't ready to do the now. George was just not here. She was still Mrs. not Widow. That was old. That was sad. That was final.

She rolled to her side looking at the space that should hold George's pillow. It was empty. She knew it would be. There was no false hope that this was just a dream. The familiar pain came. Her heart constricted, and silent tears ran down her cheeks.

As she cried silently she became aware of a strange sound.

She held her breath and listened. There it was again. A strange scratching sound. What the hell? She listened harder. Something was scratching at her camper door.

Ruby slid out of bed. A stray tear dripped off the end of her nose. Absently, she brushed it away. Within three steps she reached her camper door. She lifted the corner of the curtain that covered the door's window. It was dark out. She couldn't see anything. There it was again, a small scratch. Suddenly she remembered she had an outdoor light on the camper. She flipped the switch, looked down and laughed. George looked up at her and wagged his tail. They stared at each other. George shivered.

"Faker," Ruby said, laughing. "It's not that cold out. You've been living outside."

George cocked his ears as if he couldn't hear her or didn't understand. He whimpered, pitifully. Ruby opened the door, intending to talk to him for a second and send him back to his sweatshirt bed. The minute the door opened, George streaked into the camper.

"Wait… no… You don't belong in here. How do I know you won't pee on my floor?" George looked at her in disgust. "Oh, what the hell. Okay. You can lie on the floor over there. I suppose you want me to go outside and get your damn sweatshirt." George wagged his tail. Ruby slipped on her sandals and retrieved the sweatshirt and George's water bowl. She put the sweatshirt on the floor in front of the kitchen counter and set the water bowl next to it. George looked grumpy.

"Now what is your problem?" she asked. George looked toward the end of the camper at her bed. "Oh hell no. Not a chance. This is your bed. Take it or leave it and don't make yourself too comfortable. I haven't decided if I am going to keep you."

Looking dejected, George stepped onto his sweatshirt,

turned around three times and lay down with a sigh, his back to Ruby.

"Be that way," Ruby grumbled. She locked the camper, turned off the outdoor light and crawled back into bed.

Ruby snuggled under her covers and listened to George's steady breathing. It felt like it had been an eternity since she had heard that sound. She was shocked to realize it might have been one reason she had trouble falling asleep at night since her husband's death. The night had become so silent. Again, the empty feeling overcame her. She choked down a sob, burying her face in her pillow.

Her conscious tried to surface, pulling her from her sleep. Something important. Something different. Ruby rolled to her side and reached out like she often did in her sleep.

George smiled at her. Her husband's familiar face lit by sunshine was smiling at her. Ruby's heart soared. George, her husband, he was here. They were on a mountain, laying on a rock warmed by the dazzling sun, holding hands. He was looking at her, love shining in his eyes. They both closed their eyes, reveling in the together. The now. Ruby, content, snuggled closer. They both fell asleep in the warm sunshine.

Ruby smiled to herself. Her husband's familiar soft snore reached her ears. The rock felt so comfortable. The sun, so warm. Her husband resting next to her, snoring softly. All was right with the world. She reached to her side. She ran her fingers through his hair. George. The man she loved. With her. Not dead. Not gone. She stroked his hair, and he woke and licked her forehead.

Licked.

Not the kiss she expected.

Ruby's world crashed hard. She opened her eyes. George

was looking into her soul. Gently, he licked the fresh tears on her cheeks. George. The dog. Not her beloved husband. The dog.

Ruby sobbed.

George crawled onto her chest and put a paw on each of her shoulders. He pushed his muzzle alongside her neck under her right ear. His tongue flicked softly, kissing her neck. He pressed himself hard down onto her, giving her his best doggy hug.

Ruby's arms came around the dog and she held on as she cried herself to sleep.

"Get out of bed you flea-ridden cur." Good naturedly, Ruby cursed the dog that was sharing her pillow. The dog wagged his tail happily and licked her chin. He stood up and stretched, wincing at the soreness in his flank where the vet had given his shots. He jumped off the bed and trotted to the door where he woofed politely.

"You need to go outside?" Ruby asked. George woofed again. Ruby stood up and stretched herself. Then she crossed to the door and let George out. He trotted across the campsite and entered the woods. "Hey, where are you going?" George looked back at her and disappeared. Ruby frowned and shrugged. Maybe he was modest. She took care of her own business, giggling that she had indoor plumbing in the little tin can that was her camper.

Refreshed, showered and in clean clothes, Ruby pulled down the coffee and measured beans into her grinder. Within minutes the smell of freshly ground coffee filled the camper. The sun was shining, and she had editing and writing work to do.

Gathering her laptop and her coffee, Ruby went outside

and set up her office at the picnic table. She wasn't sure if she was going to be able to write sitting like this, but it was too nice to sit in the camper. Soon, she was lost in her work, a mocha steaming by her side.

George trotted out of the woods looking satisfied. He lapped up some water from his new water dish and looked forlornly in his food dish. He moved over to Ruby as she sat typing, oblivious, concentrating. George sat up. Ruby didn't notice. George sighed. Ruby kept working. George woofed, softly.

"Yeah, I see you're back. Good dog." Ruby didn't even look at him. She was working at a furious pace. George trotted over to his empty food dish and picked up the small metal bowl, grasping it distastefully in his teeth. He kept his lips curled, not liking the feel of the cold metal against his mouth. He walked over to Ruby with the dish in his mouth. Nothing. He sat up, looking as cute as possible. Clueless. He reared up on his hind legs, dish dangling from his mouth, his eyes woefully sad, looking pathetic as possible.

"WHAT?" Ruby said with exasperation, and she turned to look at him. She took in the comical sight. The pathetic looking animal doing his best to communicate the fact that breakfast was in order. "You ate yesterday. What else could you possible want?" She questioned. George flipped the bowl from his mouth and it landed in her lap, dog spit and all.

"Nice. Okay, hang on." Ruby saved the file and got up to feed the dog. She toasted herself a bagel and settled back at the picnic table. This isn't a bad way to work, she thought to herself. I think I could get used to this. George looked at her and wagged his tail. He woofed as if he could read her thoughts and was agreeing with the sentiment.

Chapter 15

So, does your sister still think you are gay?" Ruby asked as she handed Adam a fresh mojito. The fire was burning merrily, and George was curled up companionably at Ruby's feet.

"Who knows," laughed Adam, "but I appreciate you standing in as the surrogate girlfriend. She won't be happy until I get married and give her aunt status."

Adam took a sip of his drink and nodded appreciatively. "This is delicious."

Ruby nodded and raised her glass. "To a very nice evening. I had fun. Your sister is nice, and Rich is wonderful."

"Yep. I am lucky to have a friend. I could have another if you're interested." Adam teased her. "Without strings, of course."

Ruby furrowed her brow. George growled, softly.

"I'm sorry, Adam. If I led you on…"

"Lighten up, both of you," scolded Adam, looking pointedly at the unhappy dog. "I am just teasing, but I am curious. You never told me your story. Since you are my surrogate girlfriend, I think I have the right to know." Adam looked at Ruby and waited patiently. Ruby's head was down as she stared into her drink. When she raised her head, her eyes glistened with fresh tears.

"Oh, Ruby, I'm sorry. I didn't mean to pry." Adam reached toward her, but dropped his arms helplessly, not knowing what to do. George jumped into Ruby's lap and licked her tears. Ruby angrily brushed away the remaining wetness while George settled into her lap. Adam looked miserable.

"It's okay. It's just very hard to talk about. I lost my husband a short while ago. He passed away unexpectedly, no warning, no nothing."

"Oh shit. I'm so sorry. Was he a lot older than you?" Adam's eyes held compassion and concern. Ruby glanced up and locked eyes with him. When she saw caring instead of self-serving sympathy, she went on.

"No, a year and a half is all. He had an underlying heart condition. He must have found out about it, but never told me. He made sure I was financially taken care of so when he passed away, I would be okay."

"You're not okay, though, are you?"

Ruby shook her head. "I don't think I will ever be okay. I don't want the damn money. I just want George back."

Adam's head snapped up.

"George? Your husband's name was George?"

Ruby nodded miserably. The dog looked steadily at Adam as if daring him to be an ass.

"But you named the dog George. Do you think that's healthy?"

"No, I didn't. Remember I told you that the collar he was wearing had the name George embossed into it. Believe me, I would never have named this dog George!"

George looked up at her, his feelings profoundly hurt.

Adam was quiet for a minute. Then he spoke earnestly.

"Ruby, I lied to you."

"What, you are gay?" Ruby smiled, trying to lighten up the situation.

"No, about the dog."

"What about the dog?" Ruby set her drink down and faced Adam, her serious face full of suspicion.

"I told you that I may have seen the dog around. What I didn't tell you is that this dog has been at this campsite for the last three weeks. I haven't been able to catch him, but he wouldn't leave this site. It's like he has been waiting for something. For someone. I watched him get thinner and thinner, his coat full of burrs, but he wouldn't come to me. He wouldn't leave here, and he wouldn't eat. The first time I ever saw him come to anyone was to you. Hell, he even avoided the sweetest little girl that tried to coax him out from under the bushes. She left him an ice cream cone. He did creep out and eat that, but it's the only thing I've seen him eat. When I saw that he had attached himself to you, I hoped that maybe you could help me catch him so I could get him some care and then take him to a no-kill shelter. Once I saw the two of you together, I had the weirdest feeling you needed to take him home with you. Now I am convinced and embarrassed. I feel like I hit on you in front of your husband."

The entire time Adam was talking, Ruby stared at him with her mouth hanging open. When he finished, she took a huge gulp of her drink. She looked down at the little dog. He lifted his right paw. She shook her head and looked away, dumping the dog on the ground as she stood.

"You are nuts. This is a dog. A stray. A stray who had a collar with the name George. That's it. Nothing more. Adam, I'm sorry. I'm tired. It was a nice evening, but I feel like turning in. Please feel free to finish your drink and enjoy my campfire, but I am done for the evening.

With that Ruby picked the remains of her mojito and went

into her teardrop, leaving Adam and George sitting in front of the fire. It was their turn to have their mouths hanging open.

Chapter 16

Ruby woke up the next morning with a pounding headache. She had cried herself to sleep after throwing herself on her bed, still wearing the clothes from the night before. Now, she was suffering serious morning breath from not brushing her teeth, and her stomach hurt from where her belt dug into her soft flesh all night.

Groaning, she opened her eyes and glanced at the empty space next to her. Immediately, she felt guilty. She had abandoned the poor dog, forcing him to spend the night outside. She had never intended to have a dog, much less let him into her camper and up onto her bed, but she missed his warm little furry body. *Much like the hairy body of your dead husband, George,* a tiny voice echoed in her head. *Shut up,* she told herself. She got up and stretched. Rubbing the sleep from her eyes, she opened the camper door and looked outside, wondering where George had gotten off to.

She was surprised to see a tiny tent set up next to the dead campfire and Adam and George emerging from the zippered door. With as much dignity as possible, George stalked passed Ruby and entered the woods, not looking back at her.

"He's pissed," said Adam matter-of-factly.

"It shows. And you are, too? Why are you here?" asked Ruby.

"No, I'm not pissed. I'm here because I was worried about you, and do you know how to make coffee?"

"What, you think I am only good for exotic Cuban alcoholic wonders, but can't handle something Brazilian?" Ruby said with pretend indignation.

"No, I think you can probably do anything you want. I guess a better question, is, are you going to make coffee, or should I?"

"How are you going to make coffee?" Ruby asked, stubbornly.

"How quickly you forget. I'm an Eagle Scout, remember? I have a little backpacking stove and some coffee in my truck." Adam looked particularly proud of himself.

"Instant?" Ruby asked, the disgust barely hidden.

"So?" Adam retorted, feigning hurt feelings.

"Come on in, watch and learn," said Ruby, "But I have to brush my teeth first."

"Let me take down my tent while you brush your teeth. The sun has already dried it. Then I will be happy to see if you really know how to make coffee."

Ruby went into the camper and cleaned up quickly, changing into a fresh set of shorts and Cleveland Rocks t-shirt. She smiled at the tan she'd gained on her bare feet while working outside yesterday.

"Is it often that you grin at your feet?" asked Adam as he waited at the door for permission to come in.

"Every day," Ruby quipped. She pulled out her beans and poured them into the grinder.

"Seriously? Fresh ground? I'm in love. I realize we covered this yesterday, but I am a red-blooded American. Maybe I should just ask you to marry me. Would that work?"

asked Adam as he sniffed the air, ecstatic at the aroma of the coffee.

Ruby stiffened until she realized he was teasing and trying to break down the wall she had put up the night before. She forced herself to relax and motioned for Adam to come in.

As Ruby filled the French press with steaming hot water, she turned to Adam to apologize. He held up his hands to stop her before she could speak.

"Don't apologize. You have nothing to be sorry for. I came on too strong last night. My gut told me you were sad and hurt, but I didn't want to listen. I wanted to push because I am selfish. Ruby, I like you. I like your sense of humor. I like your toughness, and you make a hell of a mojito. But you are not in that place right now. I know that. Just like I am not in the place right now for a permanent female fixture in my life. I have to respect you as I want to be respected." Adam reached out and put his hands on her shoulders. He didn't pull away as Ruby flinched, but he smiled a comforting smile at her. "I want us to be friends… without benefits. Is that fair? You make me smile. You are an amazing person who, with a little arm-twisting, is willing to give a stray a home. You're good people. Friends? That's it, just friends?" Adam looked at her steadily, his smile warm, his eyes kind.

Ruby ducked her head and moved toward him. His arms came around her in a brotherly hug. She looked up, her eyes again misted in tears.

"Yes, friends," she said. "If this were another time, another place, things might be different. But, now, just friends." They hugged each other, then Ruby poured the steaming coffee into mugs. She slipped sandals on her nicely browned feet and they went outside in the sun.

George trotted out of the woods. He checked his water and food dish and looked at Ruby reproachfully.

"Damn it. I keep forgetting to give him breakfast," groused

Ruby. She got up from her camp chair and poured dog food in George's dish. "Do you forgive me, buddy?" she asked as she scratched behind his ears. He lifted his nose to the sky and squinted his eyes in ecstasy. All was forgiven.

"So, what is next for you?" asked Adam as Ruby settled herself back in her chair in the sun. "Where do you go from here, and how do you pick up your life?"

"I don't know," Ruby said honestly. This morning, it seemed like it was easier to talk about things, like maybe last night was the impetus she needed to face her future. "I guess I can do whatever I want. George bought me this trailer, and I think maybe I should take advantage of it," Ruby said.

"George bought the teardrop for you? You say that like you weren't involved," said Adam.

"I wasn't. I didn't know he'd done it. A couple of days after he passed, I got a phone call. The dealership wanted to know when George was going to pick up the camper. In his things, I found a brochure for this. George knew I wanted us to travel the country like gypsies once we retired. He wasn't that type of person. I have wanderlust, George liked his recliners and watching sports on T.V.. George knew me inside and out, and he understood my restless spirit. He tried to accommodate me, he really did. It was actually laughable that he tried things with me that were so obviously outside his comfort zone."

Ruby took a sip of her coffee, wrapping her fingers around the warm cup. She flashed back to the times George would hand her a cup of fresh coffee, telling her it was his warm hug. It hurt to think about it, but the cut wasn't quite as fresh, not nearly as raw as yesterday. Crying half the night must have started some kind of healing.

"George must have known his end was imminent, so he got me this trailer. The sales person told me it was easy for one person to handle. He knew I would be alone, and he wanted me to follow my dreams." Tears formed and gathered in her long lashes. "I just don't know what they are anymore."

Adam took her hand and forced her to look at him. He smiled then reached up and touched her gently under her chin.

"I think you might know what your dreams are. I think you're afraid to open your eyes and your heart to follow them. Don't you understand? George gave you permission. He gave you this camper and his blessing to follow your heart, the heart you had stifled all those years because of your love for him. Now, he wants you to fulfill that pull within you. Travel. See the country. Go where your heart tells you to go. Listen to what your gut tells you and turn your camper that way." Adam dropped his hand from her chin and picked up the dog who had just sat in front of him and was currently wagging his tail in approval.

Ruby looked at the two, an idea forming in her head. She picked up her cell phone and hit a speed dial number.

"Laney, it's Ruby."

"Hey, how are you? How's the writing going? Do you have an article for me to send out?"

"I do. I will put the finishing touches on it today and will send it by this afternoon. Also, I finished the edit on the article, *Herpes and You*." Adam raised his eyebrow at her as Ruby smiled sweetly back.

"That's great, but how are you doing?" Laney asked, concern obvious in her voice.

"Actually, I am doing well. You were right. I needed this. Laney, I've made a decision. I was wondering if I could take some time off? I mean, I'd rather keep working for you, but it wouldn't be fair, so the best I came up with is to take a leave of absence or something. I understand if you can't hold my job. I mean... I can't just expect you to."

"Ruby, for crying out loud, stop. Yes, you can have time off, but what are we really talking about? What's going on? Slow down and speak as succinctly as you write, please."

Ruby took a deep breath as Adam nodded in encouragement. He didn't know where she was going with this, but the dog seemed attentive and happy.

"I am thinking of going on the road. George bought this camper for me, so I could do just that. I enjoyed writing this article, so I am thinking about continuing that… maybe freelancing if I have to. If you were interested in keeping me on, you could send me my work, and I could edit it on the road. I really don't need to be in the office to do my job. That is something you will have to decide if you can live with, but I need to do this."

"Ruby, I think that is an amazing idea. I am completely behind you. You have always completed your work for the company, and you are without reproach. You are right, we don't need you in the office, and, if the truth be told, space is at a premium here. So, from this day forward, your camper is your office, and when you come home, you have a place here as well. We can work out the details later. Are you at least coming back one time before you take off?

Ruby laughed into the phone, suddenly feeling freer and lighter.

"Yes, I will be coming back in a day or two. We can talk about how we will structure this work agreement, and I will let you know when I am ready to go back out on the road. Laney, thank you for your understanding, and thank you for kicking me in the butt when I needed it. You are an amazing friend."

Ruby and Laney said goodbye, and Ruby looked up to see George on Adam's lap and Adam grinning happily.

"I think you made a great choice. I think this is what your husband was hoping you would do. Now, my suggestion is to honor his last wishes. Go live your life."

Ruby was still for a minute.

"Adam, he said a few things right before he died. One of the things he said was to follow my heart. He asked me to promise him I would always follow my heart. That's what I am going to do."

With that, the little dog jumped down from Adam's lap and leapt into Ruby's, showering her face with dog kisses. Laughing, Ruby wrapped her arms around the squirming ball of fur. She moved her face against his and whispered in his ear.

"Thank you, George. I will follow my heart, and you are coming with me."

Part Two

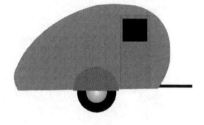

Chapter 17

H oly shit, I'm going to hit a horse, thought Ruby as she slammed on the brakes of her Jeep and reached out her right hand to grab George so he wouldn't sail through the windshield. She glanced in her rearview mirror to make sure her teardrop trailer was still behind her where it belonged. When she returned to gaze out the front window, she realized she was at an impasse. The stallion that had bolted onto the road in front of her vehicle was now standing facing her. Staring her down. Daring her to move.

George was not happy that he had been awakened from his nap in the sunshine. He looked at Ruby as if to ask what the hell was going on. She ignored him. Then he noticed a movement in front of the Jeep. The horse took that moment to give himself a hearty body shakedown, stretching his neck out like a snake and shimmying his body like a strangely shaped burlesque dancer.

George propped his front feet on the dashboard and took stock of the situation. Clearly, he needed to intervene. Ruby was just sitting there, staring. He wanted to get moving. Sitting in the hot sun in the middle of the road with no breeze blowing in his Jeep was not George's idea of a good time. Okay then. He voiced his displeasure. His sharp barking had little effect on the horse. It looked at him mildly then cocked his back right foot, taking the weight off. The horse lowered his head slightly and half closed his eyes. He switched his tail, knocking off a couple of flies.

George was fit to be tied. He was ineffective. He bounced up and down on his front paws, growling and barking, raising a general ruckus until Ruby was laughing so hard she couldn't see. It was comical to see the indignation on the little dog's face.

"George, darling," she said. "I've got this." Ruby laid on the Jeep horn, smirking at George, certain that she had solved the situation. The horse opened one eye and blinked. He stretched his nose toward the Jeep and investigated the front winch. He tasted it. George went crazy.

Ruby checked her review mirror then put the Jeep in reverse, carefully backing away from the horse. When she had enough clearance, she pulled forward to cross the center line and move around the horse. As she began to pass the stallion, he sauntered forward, then stopped in front of her bumper. George looked at her in disbelief. Ruby couldn't help but laugh at the dumbfounded look on the dog's face.

"Oh relax, George. We aren't in a hurry. We will just wait him out." She put the car in park and pulled out her camera. She was pretty excited that the wild horse was standing in front of her. After all, that's one of the reasons she had always wanted to come to Assateague Island. She had read about these ponies ever since she was a kid, and she felt like a kid, giddy with excitement that there was a stallion stubbornly blocking her way. George, on the other hand, did not have the same admiration for the beast. He was, after all, the only beast that mattered. He growled at the horse the entire time Ruby took her pictures. Then, for whatever reason, the brown and white horse decided it was time to move on. He finished crossing the road and ambled down into the brackish water that flooded the wetlands on the bayside of the island. Ruby watched as he joined the rest of his herd, grazing as he walked.

A motorhome approached, the man driving shaking his head and waving his arms at Ruby, angry because her Jeep was on the wrong side of the yellow line. There was no longer a horse in the way to explain her terrible driving habits, so Ruby shrugged an apology and George hid below the dashboard, clearly embarrassed. As the motorhome passed the driver leaned out the window and yelled.

"Stupid bitch!"

That brought George out from under the dashboard in a hurry. He bared his teeth and barked out the back window at the quickly receding recreational vehicle.

"Calm yourself, George. I don't need protecting from that guy. He has anger issues, and we will never see him again. We're almost at the beach where we can relax and drink disguised mojitos while our toes are in the sand. Well, at least I can drink mojitos. You can have water. I'll put a sprig of mint in it just to be social. What do you say?"

Ruby continued the conversation with her dog as she turned her camper into the park campground on the northeast side of the island. She stopped at the office to check-in and get her site tag. George poked his head out the window taking in all the scents of the fresh ocean air.

Pulling away from the entrance gate, Ruby felt her soul lighten. The ocean on her left was clean and sparkling, the sky a deep blue, and the air warm and salty. This was the right choice. This was the perfect place to start the journey of her new life.

Chapter 18

Ruby pulled her little trailer into her assigned campsite. She grinned as she realized there was nothing between her camper and the beach except for a protected dune. Hers was the last site on the bend of the cul-de-sac, far away from the boardwalk that led to the beach. She would have relative privacy despite the full campground.

Ruby had made these reservations six months ago, and she agonized over which site to select. Apparently, she made a good choice. George wiggled with excitement, eager to get out of the car.

"Sorry, buddy, but you have to be on a leash. The rules are very explicit, and we can't hide the fact that you are free. There is no cover here, so suck it up, buttercup." George looked disgusted as Ruby snapped the lead on his collar. They jumped out of the Jeep together and took a stroll around the site. There was a substantial wooden picnic table on the beach side of her camper and a large fire ring situated in the back of her site. Behind her was nothing but protected dunes, the beach, and the Atlantic Ocean. She was going to set up her camper fast and head to the beach. After doing absolutely nothing for the next couple of hours on the beach, she was going to start a fire, throw some food in the coals to cook, and then do absolutely nothing while sitting at her campfire. She was going to do absolutely nothing. Absolutely.

Ruby leveled the camper and set out two folding camp chairs, one for her and one for George. The dog immediately jumped into his chair, sitting on his haunches to survey his new kingdom. Ruby disappeared into the camper again and emerged a few minutes later with a refreshing mojito and a beach tote.

"Come on, George. I've got water and an umbrella for you and an adult beverage, book, and blanket for me. Today, we relax and enjoy the beach. Tomorrow, we work, then relax and enjoy the beach. Does that work for you?" The dog looked at her and wagged his tail. He jumped down from the chair and joined her on the stroll over the dunes to find the perfect spot on the sand.

R uby settled on the warm sand and stretched her toes, enjoying the feeling of being barefoot. She always was one for not wearing shoes. She shed them whenever possible. George, her deceased husband, not her dog, never understood her fascination for freedom of the feet. George liked to keep his shoes on. George, the dog lay down next to his mistress, his attention on her face. He didn't miss a trick. He knew she was missing her husband. It had been just over a year since her husband of twenty-four years died suddenly. George, the dog, came into her life shortly after.

Ruby had tried to take a leave from her editing and writing job to go on the road in the little teardrop camper that her husband had secretly purchased for her just before he died, but her boss would have none of that. They worked out a plan where Ruby would work in the office when she was in town and submit her projects wirelessly when she was on the road.

It took some time to work out the logistics. Ruby sold the house she and her husband shared. She was no longer interested in living in that space without him. She rented a small condo that she and George shared when they weren't on the road. After two small trips in her teardrop, trying out the arrangement, Ruby committed to spending the next year completely on the road. Laney, her boss, was still supportive. In fact, Laney said that Ruby was even more productive when she wasn't stuck in the confines of the office.

Assateague Island was their first stop. After that, Ruby wasn't sure. She wanted to be spontaneous, the thing that she had always wanted, but had never allowed herself to do. George, her husband, liked things planned and in their place. He liked his recliner and his football games, but he loved Ruby with all his heart, and he wanted nothing more than to make her happy. When he knew his heart condition would probably take him from her, he bought her the little camper and gave her his blessing to be free and be happy. Ruby was having a hard time with the conflict in her heart. She wanted that freedom, yearned for it, but she felt guilty, like a traitor to the husband who loved her so deeply.

A pod of dolphins skimmed through the surface, arching their backs, the sun glistening off of their dark skin. Ruby wiggled, settling her low beach chair deeper in the sand. It was time for some serious relaxing. She reached into her bag and grabbed the novel she was currently reading. Making sure the beach umbrella shaded George, she opened his folding water dish and filled it with fresh water. George thumped his tail against the sand. Then closed his eyes and settled in for a beach nap.

Ruby unscrewed her thermos and took a sip of the

refreshing Cuban mojito. Just about everything was right with the world. Just about…

"Well, hello there, pretty lady." George growled in his sleep, then opened his eyes and growled louder. The man standing at the foot of her chair stood his ground. Ruby looked up from her book and squinted, her right hand shielding her eyes from the bright sun.

"Can I help you?" she said, allowing the annoyance to show clearly on her face and in her voice.

"No, but I think I can help you. I see you are all alone here, and I would like to offer you some companionship. May I put my towel down next to yours?" George got to his feet, his tail out stiff. He curled his lips and growled again, in case the man missed it the first time.

Ruby sighed. She didn't want to be rude, but she did want to be left alone. She didn't own the beach, although it was clear that George thought he did. Maybe if she was polite, but continued to read her book, he would get the hint and leave her alone.

"It's a free country," said Ruby, in a non-committal sort of way. Then she turned her attention back to her book.

Chapter 19

"Bill Deekson."

Ruby glanced up from her book again. "I'm sorry?"

"The name's Bill Deekson, pleased to meet you." Bill Deekson extended his hand as Ruby pointedly ignored it. He continued to put down his beach towel despite the non-stop growling from George.

Ruby sighed, "George, enough. Quiet!" George gave a final growl and looked at Ruby with reproach. She rubbed his ears comfortingly. "We need to be polite." Ruby was hoping that Bill would get the hint that polite was all she was being.

"I didn't catch your name," said Bill as he settled on his towel and began to slather thick white sunscreen on his hairy chest. Ruby gave up.

"My name is Ruby, and obviously you have already met George." George lifted his lip in greeting.

"Well, Ruby, we are practically neighbors. I watched you pull in and set up. I'm across the street and down two sites. Yep, neighbors. How long are you going to be here? We can spend a lot of time together. That campsite of yours is prime real estate. We can have some nice private campfires behind your camper!" He leaned over and leered meaningfully into Ruby's eyes.

Ruby stared back trying not to think about the big white glob of sunscreen that somehow managed to hang off the tip of his nose like some errant mucus. She turned her head and went back to reading her book. Bill finished rubbing the thick white lotion all over his body, taking particular care with the bald spot on the top of his head and his slightly protruding belly button straining out of his tight beer gut. Ruby slid her eyes sideways to George. The dog was on his belly facing Bill, the look of distaste plastered all over the dog's grizzled face.

The sun beat down on the three of them, George shaded comfortably under his sun umbrella. Ruby sipped on her refreshing mojito while Bill baked in the heat. Beads of sweat formed into rivers which ran down his skin making lines in the sunscreen. The faint odor of man sweat wafted on the breeze. George lifted his head, sniffed and sneezed.

Bill raised and arm and gave his pit a hearty sniff.

"I think I'll take a dip. Want to join me?" he asked, looking hopefully at Ruby.

"No, thank you." Ruby didn't look up from her book.

Bill got up and stretched, rubbing his beer belly and probing his belly button when he was finished. He then started toward the ocean in a quick *Baywatch* jog which slowed after a few steps. Ruby watched mildly as Bill flopped in the waves.

"I should probably make my escape," Ruby told George. With as little movement as possible, so as not to draw attention, Ruby packed her book and supplies into her beach tote. She folded George's shade and stowed it, standing up as she did it. George stood up and shook. Then he stalked stiffly over Bill's beach towel. He sniffed the upper left-hand corner. Turning, he raised his leg and let out a steady stream of hot urine, soaking the corner of the towel. George looked up at Ruby and she could swear that he was laughing.

"That. Was. A. Bad. Dog." Said Ruby, but she couldn't hide the mirth in her voice.

Chapter 20

R uby was sitting in her camp chair nursing her mojito and scratching George's ears when Bill came back from the beach. He was turning lobster red, and he was scrubbing his face and sparse hair with his beach towel. As he approached Ruby's camper, a strange look came over his face. He sniffed the corner of his towel, shrugged and waved at Ruby. George growled. Ruby gave a half-hearted wave back then rose and went into her camper, hoping to avoid another encounter with her annoying neighbor. George followed her in and looked up at her mournfully.

"I know, buddy. This Bill guy could ruin a perfectly good beach stay. Change of plans, how about we go kayaking? Does that sound good?" George woofed in agreement. Ruby changed into her swim suit and quick dry shorts, grabbed a couple bottles of water and a small dry bag and locked up the camper. George happily jumped into the Jeep and they left the campground, passing a forlorn looking Bill.

Ruby drove to the bay side of the island and parked at the canoe launch parking lot. She snapped a leash on the pouting George and hooked him to her bumper hook. Then she proceeded to untie her kayak. Once it was free, she reached up and stretched on her tip toes, pulling the kayak toward her, balancing carefully. As she brought the kayak over her head, it tilted backward slightly, she shifted to catch the weight when suddenly the load lightened, and George growled.

"Here, let me help." A deep voice offered. Ruby turned her head and caught sight of the tanned, well-shaped legs and long Hawaiian print board shorts of her assistant

"Thank you. I think I could have handled it, but I appreciate your help."

"I'm grateful you didn't bite my head off. Some women get upset when someone helps them. You look perfectly capable, but I figured it wouldn't hurt to lend a hand. On the other hand, your dog just might do the honors and bite my head off instead." He leaned his head toward the now very agitated George.

"Yeah, well he doesn't like many men. Don't take it personally." Ruby shrugged and smiled apologetically, looking into this stranger's deep brown eyes. He was a medium built man, incredibly well-muscled with closely cropped hair. His smile was dazzling.

"Enjoy your paddle," said the stranger as he reached down and fearlessly scratched George's ears. George went absolutely apoplectic, but the man didn't even flinch. He grinned back at Ruby and walked away.

"George, you were rude." Ruby scolded. George stared at her defiantly.

Ruby pulled her paddles and life jackets out of the Jeep. She locked it and folded her keys and cellphone carefully in the dry bag and tied it to the bungees on the front deck.

She dragged the boat to the water and zipped herself into her lifejacket. Then lifted George onto the deck of the kayak.

"Stay put while I untangle the buckle on your lifejacket,"

Ruby muttered. George twisted his lips into a disgusted sneer. Ruby flipped the tiny life preserver over George's back. He lifted himself onto his toes, hating the feel of it. His face expressed his distaste.

"I do this because I love you," she scolded, laughing at his expression.

"I don't think he is very pleased with you."

Ruby turned to see the stranger walking back past her. He was carrying a bucket, and he waded into the bay.

"Yeah, there are a lot of things that displease him," Ruby said as she watched the stranger wade out waist deep into the water. She settled George into the cockpit of the kayak and moved it further in the water. Sliding in herself, she scooted the boat off the shore and glided effortlessly into the bay. She pulled her paddle out of the hull and checked to be sure it was indexed properly. Everything was in order. One slice of the paddle sent her shooting forward and next to the stranger.

It looked as though he was marching, then he bent over and reached under the water. A second later he pulled up a clam and dropped it into his bucket. He grinned at her.

"Dinner."

"Free dinner," she replied. "I didn't think about clam beds here. I don't know why. It makes perfect sense."

"Yep. Every time I come here, I get myself at least one free dinner. Tonight, clams and mussels. He gestured to a small hummock rising out of the water.

Ruby looked to where he was pointing. She could see the vegetation and the dark clusters that clung to it. Mussels. There for the taking. She decided that she was going to get a free meal herself.

The stranger could see the wheels turning.

"Hang on," he said as he waded out of the water. He jogged to his car. Ruby couldn't help but admire the muscles and the way they worked under his wet, tanned skin. His legs were strong, his back straight. He had broad shoulders and a nicely muscled ass. Yes, he was the whole package.

George growled.

"Oh stop. I can admire. That doesn't mean anything."

The man came back carrying a string market bag.

"Here, use this if you want."

"Oh no," protested Ruby, "I can't take that from you."

"It's not a problem. There are more where that came from. Besides, you can return it to me when you are done with it."

Ruby looked at him quizzically.

"I'm not a rocket scientist. You have out of state plates. So do I. I figured you're staying at the campground. Am I wrong?"

"No, you're correct."

"Okay, so borrow the bag, return it to me when you are finished. My name is Joe." He looked at her expectantly.

"Ruby."

"Nice to meet you, Ruby." He held out a still wet hand. She shook it and accepted the market bag.

"Nice to meet you, too. And thank you."

"No problem. I'm thirty-five."

"Um…okay…I'm a bit older than that…"

Joe burst out laughing, low and hearty.

"No, my campsite is thirty-five. So you can return the bag."

Ruby blushed, embarrassed. George stiffened and growled.

"George, hush. I'm sorry. That was stupid. Okay, campsite thirty-five. Got it."

Joe smiled and waved and started stomping his feet again. George relaxed and faced the bow of the kayak, waiting patiently for Ruby to put the boat in motion. Ruby took a drink of her water, then picked up her paddle and sent the boat skimming across the bay.

Chapter 21

Ruby paddled around for a couple of hours, enjoying the peace and solitude of the bay. She watched the shore birds fishing and saw several turtles sunning themselves on the muddy beaches of the hummocks that rose from the salty water. George alternated between napping in the sun and barking at any bird that he felt might have been a threat to his precious mistress.

Tiring of paddling, Ruby skimmed over to the closest tiny island rising from the water. The tide had come in considerably, so the mussels were covered with water and safe to harvest. She started pulling the biggest ones from the reeds where they had attached themselves. It was harder than she expected, and the shells were sharp. She stripped off her shirt, figuring her sport bra was good enough, and she seemed to be alone in the bay. She used the shirt to cover her hand like a glove. That worked better. She set about gathering a dinner's worth of mussels. She started thinking about the little tiny bottle of white wine she had in the cupboard. She really wasn't much of a wine drinker, rum being her preferred spirit, but she had some wine for cooking, and that little bottle would make a great base for cooking the mussels. She also had linguini in her pantry and some fresh garlic and basil. Maybe some pesto would be in order, too.

She put her mussels in the market bag and continued working her way back to her launch spot, stopping at each hummock on the way to gather more mussels. As she rounded the bend of the last island she nearly ran into Joe, who was bent over grabbing another clam.

He looked up at her, appraising her anew.

"You're going to burn if you're not careful," he told her, his eyes lingering on her breasts.

Ruby blushed and quickly covered herself with her now dirty, wet shirt.

"Don't cover up on my account," Joe teased. "I was only worried about your delicate skin."

Ruby smiled ruefully. He had her there. Her red hair and freckles were a clue as to how sensitive to the sun her skin was. Still...he did seem to be more concerned with checking out her breasts rather than the points of her shoulders which had received the brunt of the sun's burning rays.

"So how did you do?" Joe asked.

Ruby held up her market basket, showing him her hunter/gatherer skills.

"Nice. I got a good supply of clams, and some mussels, too."

They grinned at each other, congratulating themselves on their skills providing free food for dinner.

"So, since you have to return that bag to me, and I let you rent it for free, I have a thought." Joe leered at her comically.

Ruby laughed in spite of herself.

George growled heartily, ending with a warning bark.

"How about we pool our resources and share our meal? What do you say?"

Ruby thought about it for a minute.

"It's okay if you don't want to. No pressure. No expectations, just two strangers sharing a meal and enjoying the peace of the beach."

"Okay... you know... that sounds like a good idea."

"Your site or mine?" Joe asked.

Ruby thought for a minute. The image of Bill's sunburned skin and beer belly flashed in front of her mind. She grinned wickedly.

"Oh, mine. Definitely mine."

Joe helped her get the kayak on the top of her Jeep and they made plans for dinner at seven.

Chapter 22

R uby finished cleaning her mussels and made herself a
fresh mojito. George was sleeping on her bed, unaware
that he was going to share dinner with an intruder. The ocean
had calmed, and the waves were lapping softly at the shore. A
soft onshore breeze kept the evening cool and the biting insects
away.

She spread a tablecloth over the picnic table and weighted
each corner down with a softly rounded stone from the beach.
Then she set out her glass candle lantern. She stood back and
reconsidered. She didn't want this to be misconstrued for a
romantic evening. She had just met the guy and besides, she
wasn't ready for any kind of relationship. She felt that she
hadn't been widowed long enough to even entertain the idea,
nor did she feel any desire toward that end. She was still sad
and hurt that she had lost George, (her husband, not her dog).
She had no idea that he had a heart condition until he up and
died on her. She hugged herself, thinking about that sweet,
kind man. He loved her to the ends of the earth. In his last
days, when he knew that he may not have long, he bought her
the teardrop camper that was sitting on the beach. She had no

idea, discovering the gift only after he was dead and buried. His final act of love.

She felt a wet nose nuzzle her bare calf. Looking down, she discovered the border terrier standing behind her, looking at her with sad brown eyes.

"Hey George," she said. George whimpered and offered her his paw. Somehow, he always knew when she was sad, when she was thinking of the first George. It was really uncanny and somewhat unnerving. If she believed in that stuff, she might think that the dog was her husband reincarnated, but that was just silly.

She sighed and turned around, heading back to the camper. George started to follow then stiffened, emitting a low throaty growl. Ruby followed his gaze and spotted Bill making his way down the road, heading straight toward her camper. He was pulling a rolling cooler and carried a cheap beer in his hand. His belly led the procession.

Ruby groaned.

"You can bite him," she told George.

George wagged his tail happily.

Bill stopped just short of Ruby's driveway. She had stepped into the camper and was watching him through the window. He adjusted the waistband on his shorts and pulled down his polo shirt which was stretched out tight across his gut. His stripes were crooked. He didn't figure that out. He poked around in his nose for a minute. Satisfied that all was well, he proceeded to advance on her trailer, cooler in tow.

As Bill approached the trailer, George set up a barrage of barking and snapping. He was not a happy dog.

Ruby opened the door and stepped out, allowing George to follow her. George ran toward Bill, barking the entire way. Bill stepped back nervously. The dog stopped just short of the nervous man. Sweat broke out on Bill's forehead. Ruby waited a beat.

"George, that's enough. Leave Bill alone." Bill shifted his weight, trying not to back away, but obviously wanting to.

"Evenin', Ruby."

"Good evening, Bill." Ruby's mind was spinning trying to figure out just how to get out of the inevitable invitation. Then she smiled. Bill relaxed, and smiled too, but Ruby was looking past him.

Joe walked past Bill, carrying a market bag over his right shoulder and two wine glasses in his left hand. He leaned over and landed a kiss on Ruby's cheek.

"Ready for that dinner?" Joe asked Ruby, glancing back at Bill.

"Absolutely," said Ruby with a smile, "Would you please excuse us, Bill?" She threaded her hand through Joe's arm and guided him toward her trailer. Bill stood and stared with his mouth hanging open. George looked up at him, gave a dismissive bark, and followed Ruby and Joe to the teardrop.

Chapter 23

"I hope I wasn't interrupting anything," Joe said with an amused look on his face.

"No, thanks. I've been trying to dodge that man since I got here. The very first hour I arrived, he managed to share beach space with me. It was…uncomfortable."

"Your dog didn't seem too pleased with him, or me, either for that matter." Joe looked down ruefully at the dog who was seated between Joe and Ruby, facing Joe and growling incessantly, low and menacing.

"George, enough. For heaven's sake." George glanced over his shoulder but didn't stop his growling. "If you don't stop, I am going to lock you in the trailer," Ruby threatened.

George looked shocked. Then pissed. He stalked off, stiff-legged and jumped into his camp chair, growling softly as he did. He refused to look at Ruby. He didn't stop staring at Joe.

"That is one ticked off dog."

"Yeah, I mentioned he doesn't like men, right?"

"You did, but what did I ever do to him?"

"You exist. That's enough. So, I made some pesto, and I

have some linguini ready to drop into boiling water. What should we do with all these clams and mussels?"

"Do you have a grill?"

"I do. It's on a table behind the camper. What are you going to grill?"

"I am going to set the clams on edge between the grates. They will cook and open up, still standing. They will cook in their own salt water and you won't even need butter. Sound good? By the way, the pesto and linguini is a great idea."

"Thanks. I can cook up the mussels in some garlic and white wine. Does that work for you?"

"Absolutely. I cleaned my mussels already. Do you need me to take care of yours?"

"Nope, already done. You start on the clams, and I will get these mussels ready. Do you need anything?"

"Just someplace to put this." Joe reached into his bag and pulled out a long loaf of French Bread and a bottle of Sauvignon Blanc. "I see you are drinking a mojito. I don't know if you like wine or not, but I won't be hurt if you don't."

"I'm not much of a wine drinker. Rum is my vice of choice, but I am not averse to giving that bottle of wine a chance. I just don't want you to waste a good bottle of wine on my unsophisticated palette."

"First of all, I approve of anything with rum in it. Second, I am not a wine aficionado. Third, this is not an expensive bottle, and fourth, it is never a waste to give something a try. Sometimes you win and find a real gem." He pointed at himself. "Other times, it just sucks." Joe gestured down to the beach where Bill disappeared. "No worries on this."

Ruby smiled at him and reached for the bread and wine. She took them into the camper and returned with a grill lighter. She handed Joe the lighter and pointed to the back of the campsite, giving him a little shove.

"Start grilling, and I will get this stuff ready. Let me know if George gives you any more trouble." Ruby disappeared into the camper and dropped the linguini into the salted boiling water. She flipped a skillet onto the cooktop and pressed several garlic cloves into the pan. She sautéed the garlic in a little olive oil then added the mussels. She opened the mini bottle of cheap dry wine and poured in into the skillet with a handful of fresh basil and some black pepper. She stirred the linguini and scooped out a cupful of the pasta water, pouring it into the mussels. Then she popped a lid onto the skillet.

Ruby sliced the bread and arranged it onto a plate. She pulled a pitcher out of her cupboard, one that usually held a boatload of mojitos for an afternoon of relaxing, but instead filled it with ice and settled the wine bottle into the pitcher. She readied two plates, napkins and silverware. Joe met her at the door as she headed out to set the table. He took them from her, his face expressing his approval at the smell in the camper.

"That smells amazing."

George barked from his camp chair.

Ruby and Joe broke out laughing.

They carried everything out to the picnic table. Ruby realized she needed something for the clams. She turned to head back into the camper and scolded George again because he was still growling at Joe. She ducked into the camper and found a plastic bowl that she used for popcorn. That would work. When she came back out she was startled to see Joe sitting at the picnic table with George in his camp chair next to him. Joe was hand feeding strings of linguini to George. The dog tilted his head back and curled his lips so his fur didn't get greasy. Joe caught her eye and shrugged.

"You can't blame a guy for trying." He gave the dog another string of linguini. George looked at Ruby and had the decency to look embarrassed.

"Some protector you are. All it takes is a bribe of food and you are no longer interested in protecting my virtue."

George stopped eating abruptly. He looked reproachfully at Joe and licked his chops, the rest of the linguini string dangling from Joe's fingers. Joe placed it on the bench of the picnic table in front of the dog, then wiped his fingers on his napkin. Ruby laughed because both the boys looked guilty.

Joe poured the wine and they toasted their good luck at acquiring a free meal from the sea. They ate their dinner under the watchful eye of the conflicted dog. The wine was delicious, and the fresh seafood was amazing. At first, they were quiet, enjoying the food and the company. They found that they were comfortable in each other's presence.

Bill wandered back from the beach, his cooler bumping behind him, obviously lighter in its load. He swayed slightly as he walked. He looked over at Ruby and Joe as he passed and sneered. George barked. Bill hurried on.

Chapter 24

S ated, they sat and talked, finishing the bottle of wine. Ruby told Joe about how her husband had passed away, and Joe told Ruby how his fiancée of two years left him for a body builder. George moved closer to Joe each time Joe slipped him a piece of French bread.

"What kind of dog is George?" Joe asked as he reached out to scratch the dog's ears. George stiffened, but allowed the contact.

"The vet said he was mostly Border Terrier. Apparently, they are known for thinking for themselves. I think that translates into being judgmental!"

"I like the way he looks. Small, but tough. He certainly isn't a pushover. I had to bribe him with prime linguini and pesto to get him to just stop growling at me."

George rewarded Joe with a low growl. His lips curled, and he licked his chops with a glitter in his eye.

"I don't think he is thinking about chewing on linguini," Joe said. "I think I may have just become the main course."

"George, do you want to be locked up?" Ruby threatened.

George laid down with a disgusted thump.

"Is he really always this friendly, or is it just Bill and me?"

"In all honesty, he is very friendly to all my friends. But then, most of them are girls. He didn't like the man who came to hook up the cable in my condo. He stalked him like a lion, following the poor guy everywhere he went. I finally had to lock George in the bedroom. Then he started digging at the carpet. It's the first time I was ever mad at him. I chewed him out good. He pouted for the rest of the day."

"I guess it's good that he's protective, but what do I have to do to prove to him I have no ill intentions?'

"I don't have a clue. I wouldn't make any fast moves if I were you." Ruby grinned at him but made her point clear. Joe smiled and nodded.

"Don't worry. I have no intention of any improprieties. Not that it wouldn't be interesting." He waggled his eyebrows.

George jumped up barking. Joe laughed. George barked louder.

Ruby stood up and began to clear the table. Joe stood up to help her. The dog watched them both, carefully. As Joe carried the plates to the camper, George jumped off the chair and ran ahead, blocking the door to the camper.

"Listen, dog, I am not leaving Ruby with dishes. Now you can move aside so I can help your mistress, or you can have me move you aside. I want you to know that I am bigger, stronger and perhaps smarter than you. So get with the program or have your dignity permanently damaged."

George and Joe stared at each other, each one unmoving. Ruby shifted from foot to foot. The load she was carrying was getting heavy.

"You've got until the count of three...two... one..." George growled one last time, then turned and headed into the camper. He jumped up on the bed, laid down and watched the dish washing process like a chaperone at the high school prom.

When they finished with cleaning Joe asked Ruby if she would like to walk on the beach. She hesitated.

"Strictly platonic. No hanky panky. The sun is setting in the west soon, and the light on the beach will be beautiful. Maybe we'll see dolphins. I often see them this time of night."

"That sounds nice. Let me grab a hoodie. It feels like it's cooling off."

Ruby grabbed a sweatshirt and George's leash. George didn't look pleased.

"At least you get to come with us, goofball." Ruby reached down and tousled the dog's ears then gave his back a hearty rub. He moaned in pleasure and rewarded her with a happy dog smile.

"Wow, he can smile. I didn't think it was possible," Joe teased.

George looked at him with disgust. He sat patiently while Ruby snapped on his leash, then he led the way out of the camper.

They strolled over the dune and through the marsh grasses to the beach. They could see Bill walking in the water, his head down, his hands in his pockets. His gait seemed a bit unsteady.

George pulled on his leash and sniffed the corner of a towel left on the beach. He wagged his tail, then hoisted his leg over the shoes that were left next to the towel.

"BAD DOG!" Ruby scolded.

George laughed and wagged his tail.

Joe sniggered.

"Remind me to keep my things covered around this dog. I take it this stuff belongs to Bill?"

"That would be my guess."

They walked companionably along the beach, pausing now and then to pick up shells. Joe put the keepers in his shorts pocket for Ruby. George stopped to examine a horseshoe crab who had made his way onshore. George barked and wagged his tail, pouncing next to the helpless crab.

"Leave it," Ruby commanded. George gave a final bark and trotted up to Ruby, looking up at her adoringly. He was a good dog. She scratched his back again. George looked at Joe as if to say, *see, she is mine, not yours. She pets me.*

Joe sent a mental message to the dog. *We'll just see about that.*

George growled at Joe and leaned against Ruby's leg.

"Well, I'll be damned. The freaking dog can read minds."

"What's that?" asked Ruby, looking confused.

"Oh, never mind. Hey, look." Joe pointed out to sea. A pod of dolphins danced in the waves, making their way south along the shore. Sea birds called out above them. The evening was perfect.

They strolled further down the beach, watching the birds feasting on the small crabs uncovered by the waves. Joe looked up and pointed to a break in the dunes.

"My camper is up there. We can go up and drop off this market bag, and I can get a small plastic bag for your shells."

"What, your pocket is getting weighted down?" teased Ruby

"That and full of sand," laughed Joe.

They walked between the dunes on the boardwalk and turned right on the campground road. Two campsites later, Joe turned toward a small teardrop camper. Ruby looked surprised.

"You have a teardrop, too?"

Joe grinned and nodded.

"Why are you surprised? Do I seem like the big travel trailer type?"

"No, but not that many people have teardrops. Yours is even smaller than mine!"

"Yeah, yours is a 'standy' with the kitchen inside and a bathroom. Mine just has a bed inside. You can't stand up in it, and the kitchen is in the back under the hatch. Would you like to see?"

Ruby nodded, enthusiastically.

George grumbled.

Ruby marveled at the design of the tiny camper. There was no wasted space. Every nook and cranny had a purpose. Joe opened the door for her and she popped her head in. She thought it was going to be claustrophobic, like a coffin, but instead it was cozy and inviting, like the blanket tent she used to make as a small child. In fact, it reminded her very much of her backpacking tent, small and protective. Except her back-packing tent didn't have a flat screen TV situated at her feet, complete with a DVD player. Joe showed her the clever tables that folded down from the doors over the mattress so you could sit on the mattress and enjoy a meal while watching TV. It was absolutely charming.

Ruby popped out of the camper, and Joe led her to the back where he lifted the hatch. It revealed a tiny outdoor kitchen complete with everything you could possibly need. It actually had more room than her little indoor kitchen in her teardrop. She adored it.

"How long have you had this?" Ruby asked.

"I've been traveling in it for two years. This is my second time to Assateague Island. I love the place."

"Wait, do you live in this?"

"Yeah, pretty much."

"So, not to get personal, but how do you make a living?" asked Ruby, trying not to sound rude.

"I am a freelance photographer, and I have a house that I rent out to vacationers and to people who come into town on business. It pays the bills."

"I am also working from the trailer, but more in the hybrid sense. I go home to the office in between trips for a couple of weeks, and then I'm off again. Or rather, that's the plan. I've just started on this venture."

"So, what is it you do to pay the bills?" asked Joe.

"I edit for my company and also do some writing for them and for a travel publication. At least, that's the plan…Hey, maybe you could supply some photos of this location for the article. I can email my publisher and ask if they have a budget for that."

"Sure, just let me know and we'll see what I can produce. How do you know I'm any good?"

"I don't. I was trying to figure out how to ask you if I could see your work without you thinking I was putting the moves on you."

"Hang on." Joe opened the camper again and slid the door open on a small cupboard. From there he produced a business card. "My website is listed on this card. Go there and check out the online portfolio. If you like what you see, send the link to your editor. Let them take it from there. Sound good?"

"It sounds perfect". Ruby looked up into Joe's clear, kind eyes, and they both stood there grinning like crazy. George moved between them and leaned against Joe, trying to force him away.

"Dog, you are going to be a problem," said Joe.

George looked up at him and grinned.

Chapter 25

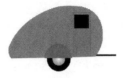

"Let me walk you back. It's getting dark." Joe tried to take the stern approach with Ruby. She wasn't having any of it.

"No thank you. I am a big girl, and I would be walking the beach tonight if I hadn't met you, so what's the difference? There is no point in you walking me to my trailer only to walk back. Besides, I have George. Who in their right mind would go up against George?"

Joe looked down at the little dog. The dog stared steadily at Joe conveying the message that he was perfectly capable of taking care of his mistress. Joe sighed.

"Well, the moon is coming up, so you will be able to see. Here take my cell phone number. If you have any problems, call me. Okay?" Joe didn't want to let her go, but he recognized that if he pressed the issue, he would just push Ruby away, and he wasn't interested in doing that in the least.

George seemed happy with that decision.

"Okay, well then, goodnight," said Ruby, suddenly uncertain as to what to do.

"Goodnight, Ruby. I had a great time tonight."

"Me, too," she said. They stood awkwardly.

George pulled impatiently on the leash in the direction of the beach.

"Take care," said Joe as he leaned in and gave Ruby a chaste kiss on the cheek when the dog wasn't looking.

George whipped around but too slowly to catch any action. He stood looking back and forth between Ruby and Joe, regarding them suspiciously.

Ruby and Joe busted out laughing. Ruby turned and lazily waved back a good night.

Joe watched them disappear between the dunes. He didn't like that Ruby was walking back without him. He didn't like it one bit.

Ruby hummed to herself as she made her way down to the water line. She liked walking in the wet cement-like sand that was the precarious border between dry feet and wet. Several times she had to dance away from the lapping waves. George snapped and frolicked in the water, happy to be alone with his mistress, although he was suspicious of her happy mood. It wasn't like her. She was usually quiet, not one for humming to herself.

Crab. George looked at the sand. Crabs. Tiny ghost crabs scooted in front of him. Oh joy! He pounced and barked and chased them as they disappeared into their holes. They didn't know that he was a terrier, bred to dig foxes out of their holes. Ghosts crabs were not foxes. Not even close.

Ruby laughed and unsnapped George's leash. There was no one else in sight, so she felt comfortable giving him his freedom. Suddenly unfettered, he ran as fast as he could away from her just inside the waterline, turned a sharp one eighty and came flying back, his ears flapping behind him. He jumped up to Ruby, barked and took off again. Back and forth the little dog ran, giddy with the freedom of being able to exercise his legs.

On one return run, his nose caught a scent and he stopped suddenly, his butt flying over his head as he rolled in the sand. He whipped around and started digging, sand flying behind him with a frenzy.

Far down the beach, Joe stood on a sand dune and watched the small shadows. He smiled at the antics of the dog. *Someday,* he thought. *Someday you will be that free and happy when I am around.*

The dog stopped digging and looked back toward the dune. He stiffened. Joe knew the dog understood he was watching them. *Good. Don't forget. I am here, and I will protect her, too. You've got a partner, buddy, whether you like it or not.*

The dog lifted his leg and peed in the sand. With dignity he came back to his mistress' side and escorted her the rest of the way down the beach to the opening in the dune that led to her camper.

Joe smiled to himself and walked back to his campsite, satisfied that Ruby was safe.

Chapter 26

R uby pulled her Ohio University t-shirt over her head and snuggled down under the blankets. The exhaust fan in the roof was running, and the windows were open, bringing the cool salty air into her camper. This was how she liked to sleep; the room cold and blankets heavy and warm.

She was tired. It was a long day in the sun, and her muscles were a little sore from the kayaking earlier in the day. George was snuggled next to her on his pillow already snoring softly. The camper was dark except for the moonlight that was lighting up the sand outside.

Just as Ruby drifted off to sleep, she heard a noise. Her eyes snapped open. She listened. There it was again. George's eyes snapped open.

George growled, deep and menacing.

Another noise, a tripping sound and swearing,

George jumped to his feet, positively apoplectic.

Someone started pounding on her camper door.

"Ruby, come on. I'm on vacation. You are, too. Why can't you spend a little time with me? I know you'll enjoy it."

Bill.

"Come on Ruby, open up. I'm a lot more fun than that douchebag that was here earlier with his fancy wine. Open the damn door."

Okay, this was not funny.

George hurled himself out of bed and stood at the door barking and growling so hard Ruby was afraid he would have a heart attack.

"Bill, go away. You're drunk,"

"I'm not drunk. I just wanna spend a little time with you."

"I said go away."

"Tell your damn dog to shut up, and let me in. We could have a lot of fun. I know you will have fun if you just get to know me. I really want to get to know you, Ruby."

Ruby peeked out the window toward the campsite next to her. There was no car with the camper parked there. The occupants must still be painting the town over in Ocean City on the Boardwalk. There was no neighboring campsite on the oceanside.

Bill was still raising a ruckus, and George was still defending his castle and his queen.

"Go away, Bill, or I'm going to call the police."

"Don't be stupid, Ruby. The police aren't going to come out here. They have enough to do in Ocean City. Just open the door, and I will be quiet. I promise. We can just talk and get to know each other. Doesn't that sound nice?"

George was barking himself hoarse.

Ruby was beginning to feel a little frightened.

"What the hell are you doing here? Get the hell out of here before I hurt you. Do you understand?"

"Go away. You already had your turn with her. Now it is…"

The next sound was that of flesh hitting flesh, then a howl from an inebriated man.

"Now get the hell away from this campsite, and don't ever come back or I will finish what I started."

Ruby held her breath. There was a knock at the door. Firm, demanding, but not erratic.

"Ruby, it's Joe. Would you like to please open the door for me? I need to know that you are okay. George, stop barking now," Joe ordered the dog firmly.

George barked one last time with a slight accompanying growl.

Ruby looked out the window and saw that Joe was standing there and Bill was nowhere to be seen.

Ruby opened the door. Joe barged into the camper and gathered Ruby in his arms, drawing her to his chest. He whispered into her silky hair.

"I knew I should have walked you back to your camper. I should never have let this happen." He pulled back from her and looked her over making sure she was okay. It was then he realized she was only wearing a t-shirt.

Ruby realized it, too.

The dog figured it out right after that.

"Don't start," Joe ordered George.

George moved between the two of them, but sat down, facing Joe.

"I'm fine. Really, I am. And if you had walked me home, the same thing would have happened. Bill didn't come over until I was already in bed. You would have been long gone by then."

Joe didn't look convinced.

"What made you come over anyhow?" asked Ruby, suddenly suspicious herself.

"I didn't like the fact that I didn't see you make it to your camper. At first, I was okay with it. I actually watched you until you walked between the dunes toward your campsite, but then I had a really uneasy feeling. I couldn't shake it. I realized that

I still had your shells, so I had an excuse to come down and make sure you made it safely home. I was halfway down the beach when I heard George barking. I could tell that wasn't his normal cranky bark, but that there was really something wrong. I started running. When I heard Bill yelling, I saw red. When I got here…well I took care of business, and now here we are."

"Yes, here we are. Would you excuse me for a minute?"

Joe looked confused.

"Would you mind turning around for a minute?" Realization dawned on Joe, and he turned his back, allowing Ruby to slip on a pair of shorts. "Okay, I'm decent."

"Believe me, you were decent before." Joe looked down. "Don't start." Joe warned the dog again.

The dog was beginning to see the light. He had competition.

"I don't know how to thank you. I was getting ready to call the police, but I wasn't sure if that was going to do any good. All of the sudden, I'm rethinking living in my trailer and traveling. I don't like being vulnerable. I need to rethink this."

"Don't worry, Ruby. This doesn't happen often. Also, women who travel alone take precautions and have different kinds of protection to help take care of themselves. We can talk about your options tomorrow. For now, you should probably get some sleep, and I should probably leave this camper before I get some of the same ideas as Bill."

Ruby recognized the hungry look in Joe's eyes. She never understood why men were attracted to women in oversized t-shirts with their hair all messed up, but it was obvious she was having an effect on him.

"Well, thank you again. Oh, yeah, do you still have my shells?" She smiled at him coyly, holding out her hand. "Or are you going to use those as an excuse again to come down to visit?"

"Will I need an excuse?" Joe asked, his eyes lit with desire.

"No, I don't think so," Ruby whispered.

"Good. I'll take you up on that. Probably tomorrow. First thing. As of now, I am going to check to make certain our neighborhood drunk is tucked safely in his camper and going to stay there. Then I am going back to my campsite. Do you need anything?"

"No, thank you. I'm good. Um...this may seem silly, but would you text me to let me know you are back in your camper? I don't think Bill can take you, but I would feel better if...you know... I knew you were safe."

"I'm flattered that you care, and of course, I will text you. Good night, Ruby."

Joe took her in his arms again, then looked down at the dog.

"Stay and be quiet."

Joe bent his lips to Ruby's and kissed her deeply. She kissed him back, feeling a twinge of guilt at the fact that she enjoyed it.

George whimpered a little and turned his back on the two of them.

Chapter 27

R uby crawled back into bed after Joe made her lock her camper, and he tested the door, twice. She was exhausted and figured she would drop right off, but sleep was elusive. George was laying on the floor, his back to her. He had never done that before.

"George, get up here."

The dog didn't move a muscle.

"Come on, buddy. You always sleep up here. Come on."

Not even a twitch from the animal.

It was more than Ruby could take. The incident with Bill, the feeling of vulnerability, the fear of someone breaking into her camper, the guilt she felt about the kiss, and now her dog rejecting her broke her down. She was tired, so she couldn't stop the tears. She closed her eyes and let the tears fall down her face to the pillow. She felt horribly alone. Why did her husband have to die and leave her? Why? It wasn't fair. They were both young. It wasn't supposed to be like this. She would gladly give up her adventures just to have him back. He was steady. He loved her. She was his life. He would have protected her.

As the tears wet the pillow below her cheek, a small tongue began to wash her face, wiping it clean.

"I'm sorry, Ruby."

She heard his voice as clear as if he were alive and laying right next to her.

"I never meant to leave you alone. I loved you with all my heart. All I ever wanted was for you to be happy. Remember, I am always here. I will always protect you. It hurts me, but I want you to be happy. Be careful, but I want you to find love again. Don't feel guilty if you know that it's right. Follow your heart. I love you, Ruby."

The dog continued to gently lick his mistresses face. Ruby slept on.

Ruby woke to sun streaming through her windows and a clattering ruckus outside her camper. Once again, George was losing it.

There was a huge crashing sound, followed by a scuffling noise.

What the hell now? Thought Ruby. She looked out the window and didn't see anything, but she could hear the sound of metal being kicked or stepped on. She looked around wildly and then grabbed her big cast iron skillet. She was done being afraid. She threw the door open and burst out of the camper. Nothing. The sound was coming from the back. She flew around the side of her camper only to come face to face with a mare and her foal. The mare was licking the grill that was now laying opened and mangled on the ground. Ruby stared.

"What exactly are you going to do with that frying pan, ma'am?"

Ruby looked up to see Joe striding between the dunes, his arms loaded with two grocery bags.

"I'd come over there to save you, but it looks like you have it handled. Although, I must say you are lucky that is a mare and not a stallion. You keep running around in just t-shirts in front of healthy men, you are going to have your hands full… so to speak."

Ruby lowered the frying pan in her one hand and tried in vain to pull down the hem of her t-shirt with the other. She was largely unsuccessful.

Joe was not a gentleman and did not come to her aid. He did help himself to a good healthy look.

George stared at him with a look of disgust but turned his attention to the horses. He was going to try his hand at herding them. As he ran at the mare, his intentions clear and barking up a storm, the mare whirled toward him, her neck snaked out and her ears pinned back. She bared her teeth and settled her weight on her hindquarters, ready to strike out with a deadly hoof.

"George, come," Joe demanded in a loud voice.

George skidded to a stop. He analyzed the situation quickly, then turned and trotted to Ruby's side with as much dignity as he could manage. The mare turned and continued licking the destroyed grill. The foal looked at George with curiosity and moved toward him.

No one moved. George slowly faced the foal. The mare stopped licking and watched. The foal stretched his neck forward, his soft nose inches from George.

The mare tensed.

George flicked out a small pick tongue and licked the foal squarely on the nose.

The foal snorted in surprise.

The mare took one step forward.

Ruby and Joe were frozen.

The foal put his nose down again. George obliged and licked again.

The foal nickered.

George whimpered in delight.

The foal put his nose to Georges' side.

Then pushed. Hard, sending George end over end across the sand.

Ruby burst out laughing.

George stood up, shook himself and stalked off, jumping in his camp chair, pretending nothing happened. The mare gave one final lick to the stove, turned and gave it a hearty kick with her back hoof. She gathered her foal and headed over the dune to the beach.

"I think your grill is toast," observed Joe.

"Ya think?"

"Yeah, I think. How did you sleep? Any more visitors other than the wild horses?"

"No, it was quiet."

Ruby suddenly remembered the voice of her husband last night. She felt her heart squeeze and twist.

"Ruby, what's wrong?" Joe's looked at her, his face full of concern.

"It's nothing. Just remembering a dream I had last night. I'm sorry. I am just unsettled this morning. That's all."

"Should I leave?" He looked mournful when he said it.

George thumped his tail against his camp chair.

Ruby looked at George, conflicted. The dog stopped wagging his tail. He sighed and jumped down from the chair. He walked stiff-legged over to Joe, sat in front of him, and reached out his right paw.

"Well, I'll be damned," said Joe, as he gravely shook the paw.

Tears leaked from the corners of Ruby's eyes.

Chapter 28

"Okay, how do you feel about chorizo and eggs wrapped in a warm flour tortilla with melted cheddar cheese? Sound like an okay breakfast?" Joe held up his shopping bags as Ruby emerged from her camper dressed in something more modest than her Ohio University t-shirt. "You look nice, but I really liked the other outfit better." Joe wagged his eyebrows at her.

"Breakfast sounds wonderful. How can I help?"

"By sitting in the sun and relaxing. I've got this. What did you do with that lethal weapon frying pan you were wielding earlier when you were going to take on that momma wild horse?"

"It's in the cupboard under the stovetop. What else do you need?"

"Nothing, I think I found everything else."

Ruby smiled and sat in her camp chair, warming her face in the early morning sunshine. George jumped up into her lap. She reached down and scratched his grizzled ears. Then she reached her hand around and cupped him under the chin, bringing his face around to look him in the eyes.

"Hey, buddy. Is this okay? I mean, this isn't going anywhere. He will go his separate way and so will I. I am not going to jump into bed with him. We are just friends, sharing food and friendship. Is that okay with you?" She searched the dog's eyes, waiting for something.

George blinked and held very still. They locked eyes for a minute.

Joe came to the camper door to ask a question but spotted the two of them gazing into each other's eyes. It was like there was an unspoken conversation going on. He eased himself back into the camper.

George stood on Ruby's lap and raised both front paws to her shoulders. He licked her cheek and then moved in for a hug. Ruby put both arms around her dog and held him close. For the umpteenth time in twelve hours, tears ran down her face.

Joe came out of the camper carrying a heaping bowl of chorizo and eggs and a plate of warm flour tortillas. Ruby jumped up to help. She quickly grabbed the tablecloth Joe had under his arm and spread it on the picnic table. As he set down the feast, she went inside and grabbed plates, glasses and the orange juice Joe had left on the counter. She spied a little bowl of plain scrambled eggs sitting next to the stove. She grabbed it, too, wondering what it was for.

"Oh good, you got George's breakfast," said Joe

"Oh no. George doesn't get people food."

"Eggs aren't people food. They are every animal food. Look he likes them."

George was already diving into the unexpected treat. He lifted his head and licked his chops while looking at Joe and wagging his tail.

I told you I would win, thought Joe as he looked down at the little dog.

George grumble growled, but still wagged his tail a little. George was warming, but not yet ready for a truce.

"Whatever," said Ruby, digging into her burrito. "This is delicious. Where did you learn to cook like this?"

"My dad taught me. We used to have this every Saturday for breakfast. It was a tradition."

"That sounds nice."

"It was. Did your family have any traditions like that?"

"No. We didn't." Ruby's demeanor made it abundantly clear that this wasn't a welcome road to travel.

"I don't know what you have planned today, but I need to hike to the other end of the island. I want to get some photos of Assateague's 'wild side'. I am hoping to get some good wild horse pictures without campers or destroyed grills in them. Would you like to tag along? You might get some good ideas for your articles."

"Sure, I'll go. Do I need anything special?"

"Do you have a small backpack?"

"Sure, and I have a collapsible water bowl for George."

"Good. We need to carry water, because there isn't any fresh water to drink. Either wear or pack a long-sleeve shirt and pants. Once we get off the beach, the mosquitoes and flies can be brutal! I'm going to get my gear. I'll meet you back here in an hour and we can head out. Will that be okay with you?"

"Yep, that will work. That gives me time to shower and pack up. The sky is full of clouds, that should help with the heat and give you better light for your pictures, won't it?"

Joe looked up, assessing the sky.

"Yeah, I think it will cut some of the harsh light. I don't think we will need rain gear, but if you want to err on the side of caution, pack a rain jacket. See you in an hour."

Joe gave Ruby a peck on the cheek and patted George's head. George tolerated the affection. Joe laughed and headed through the dunes.

As Ruby turned to go back into her camper, George started growling. She looked down the camp road. Bill was making his way to the beach. He was lugging a new low beach chair, a cooler, and the towel that George had anointed. When he passed Ruby, he nodded at her stiffly. She noticed that he had an impressive shiner. *Serves you right*, she thought. She smiled, thinking of Joe protecting her. That was kind of hot.

There it was again. That twinge of guilt.

Chapter 29

They spent the afternoon hiking down the beach, heading toward the state line where Maryland becomes Virginia. After they passed an area of off road vehicles which were set up for surf fishing, the beach became desolate. They were the only ones anywhere in sight. Sea birds whirled above their heads in search of food, and small herds of wild ponies roamed the shore.

"Look at that!" Ruby pulled at Joe's arm, tearing him from photographing a group of plovers running from the lapping water. She pointed to a group of horses. They were led by a paint stallion and they were running full bore toward them, splashing through the waves at the water's edge.

Joe swung his camera up and began shooting. They held their ground, hearts beating wildly as the herd thundered past them, water spraying in every direction.

They were laughing and looking at the digital images Joe had captured when they felt the ground tremble. They turned and looked behind only to discover the herd pounding their way back the way they came, once again led by the magnificent paint stallion. His mane and tail flew tangled in the wind, his nostrils were flared, taking in all of the scents. He turned his head as he passed them, his eyes challenging George.

George hid behind Joe's legs.

"The dog has better sense than I thought." Joe reached down and picked up the dog, feeling him tremble with fear. George desperately tried to look dignified and calm. He wasn't fooling anyone. Joe deposited the embarrassed dog in Ruby's arms. She loved him for a minute before she sat him back down on the beach.

"Hang on a minute," she told Joe. She opened her pack and pulled out the collapsible bowl. She poured a small amount of water in it. George lapped it up greedily. Ruby took a long swallow out of the bottle herself. "The salty air really makes me thirsty. I wonder if it is harder on George being closer to the ground. I wonder if the air is saltier near the sand. I know that sounds silly, but he is really thirsty." She gave him another drink.

"Well, I know the air contains droplets of salt water. Either way, I'm glad you thought to give him some water. We are going to cut into the mainland soon. The island is only a mile across, so we don't have far to hike to get to the bayside, but there is a potential for biting insects, including ticks. Now is as good a time as any to zip on your pant legs and put on your long sleeve shirt."

Ruby grabbed her clothes and covered up. She pulled a zipper lock bag out of her backpack and produced a flea and tick collar for George.

"I don't like to use this all the time, but I think this might be a good idea."

Joe nodded his approval.

Once they were all covered up they turned off the beach and headed inland. There was a faint trail that they followed which lead through some marsh areas with brackish water. Joe took more pictures of horses, and some close-up pictures of some wildflowers and marsh grasses. Ruby followed behind watching him work. She enjoyed watching his graceful movements while he was taking pictures. It was like he was involved in an intricate dance with his subject, the light, and his camera.

George spent his time sniffing around. He would catch a scent and follow the trail for a little bit, but never straying too far from Ruby. Once he found something dead and took great joy in rolling in it. This was not the first time he had done this. He knew Ruby didn't share his joy in the smell of deceased animals, but he surely did. He knew when he trotted up to her, she would wrinkle her nose and say *Ewww, you stink*. She did not disappoint him.

They reached a backcountry campsite. Ruby took notes as to the amenities, not many, which were available, and Joe took some pictures of the area. Then he reached into his backpack and surprised Ruby with an impromptu picnic.

"What's this?"

"Well, this is a ham sandwich, and these are barbecue potato chips."

"I mean when did you do this? I didn't know we were having a picnic. I would have contributed."

Joe smiled at her and lifted her chin with his outstretched index finger.

"Believe me, you are already contributing." Ruby blushed. "I would have had to do this all by myself if you wouldn't have come. Normally, I'm okay with that, but today, I like what you add to the scenery. So… ham or ham?"

"Hmmm. I guess I'll take ham."

They sat down on a weathered picnic table and enjoyed their meal. George trotted off to explore the area.

The winds began to pick up, and the air suddenly chilled. Joe looked to the west and studied the sky.

"I think we'd better get going. It looks like a storm is blowing in."

Ruby looked up nervously at the sky. She thought of the long walk back to the teardrop.

"You don't think it will hit before we get back, do you?"

"I don't know. Why, are you nervous?"

"I'm not afraid of a little rain, but I don't relish being the lightening rod on the beach."

"You've got a valid point. However, I'm taller, so you should be good."

He took that opportunity to lean in and kiss her gently on the lips.

"I'll take care of you, don't worry."

"Hmmm. What about George."

Joe thought for a moment. Ruby looked sternly at him.

"Okay, and your little dog, too."

Ruby laughed then surprised herself by kissing him back.

George watched from the edge of the marsh.

Chapter 30

A dejected dog made his way, limping over to Ruby and Joe. His ears were down, and his tail held listlessly. He stepped gingerly on all four paws.

"What is the matter with you, buddy?" asked Ruby, very concerned.

"Do you think he saw us kiss?" asked Joe

"Don't be silly. Why would that make him look like this?"

Joe looked at the dog. The dog stared back, unblinking. *Oh, we are back to that again, are we?* Thought Joe. He swore the dog smirked at him.

"Joe, look at his paws!? Ruby held up a tiny front paw. Embedded in the hair between his toe pads were lots of tiny burs. "That really has to hurt."

The dog looked at Joe reproachfully. Ruby looked at Joe accusingly. Joe felt guilty. *You planned that*, Joe thought. The dog actually grinned.

"Aw, poor George." Joe sympathized. "Look buddy, I saved you a bite of my sandwich."

Boom, thought Joe. That should make you feel guilty. The dog yawned and held his paw up higher. He even managed a whimper. Then he licked his chops looking pointedly at the bite of sandwich.

Damn, thought Joe. *You are an artist, a genius.* The dog bowed his head slightly, then licked his paw to cover the movement.

George sat patiently, looking appropriately pained as Ruby and Joe worked to dig the burrs out of the dog's paws. Occasionally he would whimper and quickly lick the hand that was pulling the bur that hurt. At first Joe thought the dog was still pulling some shit, but then he realized that the dog's paws really got beaten up. Even George gave up the game while they worked on him.

"I think we got them all, don't you?" ask Ruby as she worriedly looked over all for paws.

"I don't see anymore." Joe scrutinized the bottom of George's feet as he lay sprawled on his back on the picnic table, his feet waving in the air.

"Wow, the wind has really picked up. I feel like there is sand in my teeth." Ruby spit delicately and looked embarrassed.

"Spit all you want. I feel the same way. Come on, George. Are you better? Can you walk?" Joe looked at the dog expectantly. *I'm really not expecting you to answer. I am actually asking a dog questions.*

George laughed at him, his smile wide and his tongue hanging out. The dog looked back at Joe, still laughing as Ruby lifted him from the picnic table to the ground.

Ruby and Joe shouldered their packs and checked the area for any debris they may have left. Everything looked good, so they headed down the trail back toward the beach.

George took two steps and sat down. He lifted his front right paw and licked it. He looked after them and tried to walk again. He whimpered. He looked dejected. He looked embarrassed.

You really are hurt, aren't you buddy. Don't worry, pal. I've got you.

Joe walked back to the dog and picked him up. George stiffened and curled his lip. Joe stared at him.

"Don't you dare, dog," he commanded. George lowered his lip, and they set off with Ruby in the lead and Joe carrying George.

By the time they reached the beach, the wind was howling. It was difficult to stand against it, and the sand was pelting into their skin.

"Over here. Duck behind this sign." Joe commanded Ruby.

They got on the lee side of the sign, which effectively blocked the wind.

"Put on your sweatshirt and your raincoat to help protect you from the sand. Do you think George will tolerate me carrying him in my backpack?" asked Joe.

"It's worth a try. He looks miserable."

They both quickly donned extra clothing and Joe gently placed George in his backpack. The dog seemed to know what was going on, because he tolerated it fairly well. Joe left the pack unzipped enough for the dog to stick his snout out the side.

"I unzipped the side away from the wind, so he can look out and hopefully not get his eyes filled with sand. Are you okay?" asked Joe

"Yep, let's get going. Do you think we can beat this before the skies open up?"

"I doubt it, but let's give it a try." He had to yell to be heard above the wind.

They hurried along the beach, their heads down trying to protect their faces. George settled down into the backpack bracing himself against the jarring of each step. There was a brilliant flash and a crack of thunder that made them both jump. The air was filled with electricity. George barked and whined.

"That was really close!" Ruby yelled. She was getting scared.

"Look, we are almost at the ORV area. Someone is waving at us."

They ran toward a truck where a man was leaning out the driver's side window gesturing for them to hurry. Just as they reached the truck the rain started. It pelted them like sharp needles. Joe swung the backpack off his back and cradled in it his arms. The man opened the back door of his truck and Ruby and Joe dove in.

"Oh, my goodness, thank you," said Ruby.

"You're welcome," said the driver. He was a young man, probably in his early twenties, and working hard at growing a full beard. A smiling face peeked over the seat on the passenger's side.

"We saw you guys on the beach. That lightning bolt was so close to you. You were almost hit."

"I really appreciate you helping us. My name is Joe, and this is Ruby." There was a bark from the backpack. "Oh, and this is George." Joe unzipped the backpack and George pushed his head out, trying to look dignified.

"I'm Scott, and this is Bree." Bree ducked her head and smiled.

They made friendly conversation as the rain came down in sheets and the truck was buffeted by the wind. After a half an hour the rain began to let up and the wind had died down to a gentle breeze. The sun peeked from behind the clouds, brightening the day again.

Scott started the truck and turned it around, heading back toward the air station. Joe helped him fill his tires with air, and Scott drove them back to Ruby's trailer.

"We are heading to Hooper's for crab this evening for dinner. Hooper's is always more fun with friends, ya want to come?" asked Scott. Bree bobbed her head in agreement.

Joe looked at Ruby, his left eyebrow raised. She shrugged and nodded with a smile.

"Sure, we would love to come. What time?"

They made arrangements to meet at the restaurant in Ocean City, and Scott and Bree left.

"Come on in the camper and get dry," said Ruby.

"I can't believe I am going to do this, but I am going to turn you down. You're going to get enough sand in your camper with you and George. You don't need mine to boot. I'm going to head back to my trailer and get cleaned up. I want to make sure my camera equipment is dry and in one piece after George rode on it for this afternoon's hike. I will see you later." Joe kissed her on the lips, lingering.

George made a coughing sound that ended with a hack.

You are an ass, thought Joe. George smiled at him, demurely then turned and led Ruby into the trailer. She looked over her shoulder and blew Joe a kiss. She walked into the trailer feeling like she missed out on something. She really didn't want Joe to leave.

Chapter 31

R uby stepped out of her tiny shower and checked the sundress she had hung on the door. It was a wet, but the wrinkles looked like they were disappearing. Living in a tiny camper was great most of the time, but the storage was sparse, and her clothes were always wrinkled.

She opened the camper door and leaned out, hanging her sundress on her awning to dry. Bill was walking back from the beach at that very moment. His eyes slid over her towel clad body. His eyes narrowed. He licked his lips then saluted Ruby.

Ruby slipped her arm back into the trailer and eased the door shut. Her stomach felt sick. She didn't like the way Bill looked at her. He obviously didn't get the message that Joe had sent him. She would have to watch her back.

She spent a few minutes putting on her makeup and carefully dried her auburn hair. Satisfied, she set about finding her skinny teal flip flops. The were a perfect match to her flowered sundress.

She found herself humming as she got herself ready to go out. It had been a long time since she felt this…light.

Ruby looked out the window, making sure Bill was nowhere

in sight then reached out again to retrieve her dress. It was mostly dry, thanks to the breeze off the ocean. She slipped it over her head and checked herself one more time. Reasonably happy with what she saw in the mirror, she added a spritz of perfume.

George watched from the bed, suspicious.

"Come on, buddy. Let's go outside and go potty."

George jumped up, happy. He was very aware that Ruby was getting ready to go somewhere. He had been waiting for her to get ready. She usually never took this long. Happy that he was finally called, he hopped down from the bed and stretched, a happy dog smile on his face.

Ruby opened the door and reminded George to do his business. She always told him to do his business before they got in the car. Dutifully he trotted over to some sea grass at the edge of their campsite and lifted his leg. He turned his head away from Ruby. It was hard to get any privacy around here.

Finished, he trotted back wagging his tail, tongue lolling out the side of his mouth. He gently reared up on his hind legs and placed his front paws on Ruby's hips. He smiled happily at her and accepted the ear scratches she was handing out. Pure ecstasy.

Ruby looked at her watch. She was ready a half an hour early. She could walk down the beach and enjoy the early evening sun, surprising Joe at his camper. That was better than sitting around her trailer getting anxious.

"Okay, George."

He was expecting a "let's go."

"Go back in the camper, and I'll get you a treat.

What? The camper?

George's ears slid down his head, and his tail drooped.

"Aw George, don't look like that. I can't just leave you in the car while I have dinner. I won't be long. You're tired after today anyway."

George looked at her, accusingly.

Ruby felt guilty.

George knew it. He used it.

"George..." Ruby said softly. She sounded sad.

That made George sad. He stared at her and sighed. He hopped up into the camper, refused the treat she offered, and jumped up to his pillow. He curled up, his back to Ruby, and shut his eyes. His feelings were hurt.

Ruby closed the door and headed to the beach. Her flip-flops dangled from her fingers as her bare feet made their way through the silky sand. George's attitude bothered her. He had been left behind before. She didn't take him grocery shopping or when she dined out. He never liked being left behind, but he was never a brat about it. The darn dog was almost human.

The dog hated men, especially men who showed any interest in her. The dog didn't need to worry. Ruby wasn't looking for a relationship. She had loved her husband. She honored his memory. He was so good to her and loved her deeply. He knew her secret hopes and dreams, even though she didn't know he knew. He bought her the little camper so she could fulfill those yearnings. No, she wasn't looking to replace that love.

She thought about the dog. He was so much like her husband. So happy to be settled in his chair. So happy to just be near Ruby. So happy to be settled.

Ruby stared out at the ocean, watching the waves come in. Steady. Never ending. What if the dog was her husband? What if George came back as a dog.

Ruby laughed out loud at her crazy wandering mind. She was nuts. She shook herself and started walking again. She was feeling guilty because she was going out to dinner with a guy, a friend. She was just going out to dinner with a friend. A very good-looking friend. Actually, a very hot friend.

She stopped in her tracks and looked out at the ocean

again. A pod of dolphins was playing just past the surf zone. She watched them for a moment. Thinking. *Yes, Joe is hot. He is a friend. I am a woman. I am allowed to enjoy myself and have a good time this evening. I am an adult. I am allowed to adult...*

I may not be ready to adult.

But I am allowed.

With that Ruby headed up the beach between the two dunes toward Joe's camper. Her step was lighter. Her thoughts free.

Chapter 32

"Hey, lady. You look beautiful. I was going to come get you." Joe admired the way the sundress clung to Ruby's curves and exposed her shoulders and cleavage. He imagined tracing her freckles with his tongue.

Ruby was looking down, putting on her flip-flops, so she missed the desire lighting up Joe's eyes.

"I was ready early, and I wanted to walk down. The beach is so peaceful after the storm."

Ruby failed to mention that she didn't want George to see her leaving with Joe. It would make her sound insane.

Good, thought Joe. *I don't have to have that dog stare at me as I leave with his lady. Damn possessive cur.*

"Great. Let me grab my keys and we'll go." Joe picked up the keys from his kitchen counter and closed the back hatch. He led her to his truck, opened the door and helped her up. As he closed the door, he leaned in and stole a quick kiss. Ruby looked startled, but then smiled.

"What was that for?" she asked.

"Just because I wanted to. You look so pretty."

Ruby blushed and smiled.

"Thank you. You look pretty good yourself." She slid her eyes over his close-fitting shirt and khaki shorts. His short sleeves were cuffed, accentuating his well-formed biceps. When he walked in front of the truck she admired the way his shorts fit his ass. Yes, he was hot. There was no doubt about that.

Hooper's parking lot was crowded. Joe slipped his hand into Ruby's as he led her into the restaurant. He spoke to the hostess and she led them through the restaurant and out onto the covered dock that overlooked the bay. Bree saw them and waved.

Once seated, Ruby picked up the menu. The options were staggering. Bree looked at Ruby and laughed.

"Honey, if you've never been here just jump in feet first and go with the all you can eat crab feast. It's pricey, but it's messy and fun and delicious. That's what we always get."

Joe looked at Ruby, his eyebrows raised.

"Are you game, because I sure am."

"Sounds great. Let's do it."

"Look, Ruby, they have mojitos. Are you going to have one?"

Ruby looked out over the bay and thought for a moment.

"I don't think so. I generally don't order mojitos out. Bartenders hate making them, and usually they don't do them well. Mojitos are a drink long looked down upon. I think I'll be normal and have a beer."

Joe ordered for them and they settled in, getting to know their new friends. Before Ruby knew it, the waitress approached with a huge amount of food and set it on the paper covered table. There was shrimp, chicken, Maryland blue crabs, hush puppies, and corn on the cob, all dusted with Old Bay Seasoning. Ruby's mouth instantly began to water.

"Prepare to get messy all the way up to your elbows," laughed Scott.

The conversation stopped as everyone dug in. The beer

flowed. and the food kept coming. After an hour, they started to slow down.

"That was wonderful," Ruby said, glad she wore a sundress that didn't have a waistband.

The waitress cleared the table of food, and they ordered a last round of beer. Joe sat back in his chair and absently covered Ruby's hand with his, gently rubbing the back of her hand with his thumb.

Bree noticed.

"So, you said in the truck when we rescued you guys on the beach that you just met a couple of days ago. Summer vacation romance or what?"

Ruby blushed, and Scott tried to hush Bree.

Joe didn't move his hand.

"We um, are just friends." Ruby stammered, not sure how to answer the question. She started to pull her hand away, but Joe tightened his fingers very gently over hers.

"Let's just say that we hit it off and share some interests. We're just getting to know each other, and she recently gave me permission to hold her hand. I like doing it, so I am. That's about where we stand." Joe's eyes twinkled, and Ruby ducked her head, using her beer as an excuse to break eye contact.

Bree squealed with laughter.

"You guys are all about each other and you don't even know it. Don't waste something that might just be right," she counseled.

"Aren't you awfully young to be so wise?" asked Ruby, teasing Bree.

"I am an old soul. I've been around a couple of times."

Scott snorted.

"Bree firmly believes we get several chances to get things right in life. If we screw up the first time, or miss our opportunities, she thinks we get reborn in another body. Bree believes in second chances."

Everyone laughed, but Ruby flashed back to her walk to Joe's on the beach. The weird thought that her dog was her dead husband come back to her.

Joe spoke up.

"Do you think people can come back as dogs?"

Ruby looked at him in surprise. He winked at her.

"I don't know. Maybe...why not?" replied Bree.

"Clear as mud," Scott quipped. Then he changed the subject. "We're going surf fishing tomorrow if you'd like to join us. I have extra gear if you need it."

"Maybe. We'll let you know," said Joe as they settled up the bill.

Chapter 33

O n the ride back to the campground they were quiet. It was comfortable, each lost in their own thoughts. Joe twined his finger's in Ruby's as her hand rested on the truck seat. She sighed, enjoying the sensation.

"Would you like to stop at my camper for a drink? I don't know if I'm ready for the evening to end, nor am I ready to be in the close proximity of your neighbor, Bill."

Ruby remembered Bill walking past her trailer, leering at her. She readily agreed.

Joe went and opened his kitchen hatch and pulled two beers from his ice box. They sat under his side tent awning and watched darkness fall over the ocean.

"So, are we just friends then?" asked Joe. He looked at her intently.

"We hardly know each other. We had a chance meeting and then we will go our separate ways. I only have my camp-site for three more days. How about you?" Ruby sounded exasperated.

"I only have mine for two."

Ruby's heart fell.

It surprised her.

"I guess we will have to say goodbye the day after tomorrow then," murmured Ruby. She felt defeated somehow.

"Not necessarily." Joe picked up her hand, his fingers stroking the thin skin on her wrist. "I head to the Florida Keys next. You could come with me."

Ruby sat stunned. The thought hadn't occurred to her.

"Um, I don't know. I hadn't thought about going to the Keys. I…"

"I thought you said that all your life you wanted to be spontaneous. You wanted adventure. It sucked, the way you were set free, but here you are. Here is your chance to just follow your heart. Why don't you do it?"

His fingers trailed up to the inside of her elbow, causing her to shiver.

Ruby stared off over the dunes.

"Tell you what, don't give me an answer now. Think about it. There's time. Just listen to your heart, let yourself go, and live for you."

Ruby stiffened as his hand trailed up to her shoulders, then stroked the side of her neck and along her jaw.

He dropped his hand and rose, giving her a soft kiss on her lips.

"Wait here." He closed his hatch and opened the tiny camper door. He emerged with a blanket, the kind that you can find for sale all over the boardwalk in Ocean City.

"Remind me to go to the boardwalk tomorrow to get one of those. I love them."

Joe nodded and pulled her up out of her chair. He led her toward the beach. It was dark. There were clouds covering the sky. There were no stars, no moon.

He spread the blanket on the sand behind a dune. The breeze was gentle, and the sound of the ocean lapping the shore was peaceful.

They laid on their backs, side by side staring up at the sky. Occasionally, there would be a break in the clouds and they would catch a glimpse of the stars hidden behind the fluffy curtain.

Joe raised himself on his elbow and looked down at Ruby.

"I meant what I said. I would love it if you would come with me. No commitment, just traveling together. You have your trailer. I have mine. You would have your own space. You can do your work from wherever, so that's not a reason. I have an assignment to photograph a hotel down there. Plus, I want to add to my portfolio, so I plan on spending some time just taking pictures of the area and the wildlife."

He trailed his fingers along her jawline and softly traced her lips. He cupped the side of her face and brought his lips to hers.

The kiss was gentle, chaste. He was testing her.

She felt a quickening in her loins. He was teasing her.

She kissed him back.

Carefully.

He deepened his kiss, parting her lips with his tongue, exploring, not demanding.

She sighed.

He took it as a sign.

He gathered her into his arms, lifting her shoulders off the blanket. He kissed her with more urgency, Ruby hesitated. He gathered her glorious auburn hair into his right hand while supporting her with his left. He pressed her back against his hand as his mouth worked down the side of her neck to the dimple at the base of her throat.

His tongue flicked out as he kissed her ear, then tugged on her earlobe with his teeth. Gently, ever so gently. Pressing her back onto the blanket, his hand traced the strap of her sundress where it joined at the bodice. Moving down, he palmed her breasts. Ruby responded by arching into his hand, pressing the hardening nipple against him. Ruby reached her arms around Joe. His back was strong, well-muscled. She liked the feeling of strength below her hands. Her mind flickered back to her husband. He was softer, more sedentary and his body showed it. She felt another twinge of guilt in her mind, but her body was responding to this strong, attractive, kind man. Joe shifted sideways and drew her body against his, her back pressed against his front. His erection firmly wedged against the crack of her butt.

Both of his hands were exploring the material of her dress, feeling the points where the hardened nipples strained at the fabric. He moved his right hand down to her flat stomach and slid to the dent along her hip bone. It was one of his favorite places.

Ruby's breath was coming quicker, and she pressed against his erection. She shifted slightly, unconsciously letting her legs spread apart, allowing space for his probing hand to explore.

Joe nuzzled her hair, her neck, all the while kissing her, suckling her, gently using his lips to arouse her every nerve.

His hand moved to the v of her thighs. He stopped. Teasing, testing.

Ruby's body arched forward of its own accord. Her mind was slipping into a place where there was no thinking, no worrying, no consequences. Her body wanted to be touched, and Joe was doing an amazing job.

Carefully, Joe lifted the hem of her dress and ran his hand up the inside of her thigh.

Ruby's breath hitched. He slid a finger inside her panties.

He pressed against her, waiting…Ruby responded, moving forward against him.

He teased her, worked her, and when she was just about ready to explode, he slowed down and eased her onto her back.

She was quivering. Murmuring, begging him not to stop.

She spread her legs wider, desperately urging him to go on, to touch her and stroke her to her climax. He waited.

She went wild. She rose to him, crashing her lips to his. She forced her tongue in his mouth, probing, exploring. She put both hands on the sides of his head, twining his hair in her fingers and pulling his lips to her straining breasts.

He pulled the straps of her sundress down and freed her. One hand teased and rolled her left nipple while his mouth ravaged her right.

She was panting, writhing, arching her body with need.

He looked her in the eyes.

"You are so beautiful."

Ruby came unglued. She thrashed and moaned crying out into the night, seeing the stars that were covered with clouds.

Chapter 34

Joe walked Ruby along the beach back towards her camper, their hands clasped. As they reached the boardwalk through the dunes that led to Ruby's camper, Joe caught her up in his arms again, kissing her deeply.

"I don't want to do that in front of George," he said. "You know how he gets."

"I do. He would not be a happy dog. I feel badly."

"Why?"

"Well, I don't think our evening ended the way you were hoping."

"Ruby, even if that couple wouldn't have stumbled upon us, we still would have ended there."

"Why? Didn't you want…"

"Shhh." He pressed his finger to her lips. "Tonight was about you. I wanted this for you. Besides, I'm hoping you will think about it and come back for more." He kissed her, and they walked on to her camper.

George didn't greet them at the door.

George didn't get up.

George didn't look at them.

George was pissed.

"Hey George. How are you feeling after your harrowing afternoon hiking and riding in my backpack?" asked Joe. Although he knew how the dog was feeling.

George did not respond

"Don't let him change your mind about seeing me again," Joe teased. "And think about what we talked about."

George growled from his pillow, still refusing to look at them.

"Get over it, buddy," Joe said. "Get used to the fact that I like your lady."

George growled even deeper, threatening. Then he turned around and stretched out, covering Ruby's pillow with his body, claiming her. He stared at Joe and raised his lip. Joe just laughed and saluted the dog. He took Ruby in his arms and laid a loud satisfied kiss on her lips.

He walked out the door leaving a stunned lady and dog.

Ruby got ready for bed, pulling on her t-shirt. George was still pouting on her pillow.

"George, you have to go outside and go potty. Let's go."

George didn't move.

"Seriously, I want to go to bed. Get up and get outside."

Again, George just stared at her.

"Okay, I am starting to actually get angry with you. Get your butt of my bed and get yourself outside and do your business. NOW!"

George sneered and hopped off the bed. He walked passed Ruby with as much dignity as possible. She opened the door and he trotted over to the edge of the campsite. When he was finished, he came back in the camper, still not looking at her.

"Remind me to pick that up in the morning," she told him. She reached into the cupboard and got a couple of treats for the dog. George refused to take them.

"Fine. You know what? You just be that way. I'm sorry. I

had a good time. No... I had a great time. I got to enjoy myself with a nice man who made me feel special. He is kind and good and smart, and I like him. You can either accept that fact and enjoy the next couple of days with us, or you can be a miserable dog, because I am going to see him again. End of story."

Ruby got into bed and turned her back on the little dog. He was standing on the floor looking conflicted. His tongue darted out, and he delicately snagged the treat laying on the floor. He crunched it and thought. He licked up the crumbs and hopped up in bed with Ruby, tucking his nose under her chin. She reached out and threw her arm around her dog.

"I love you George. Don't forget it."

Chapter 35

R uby woke to George licking her chin, urgently. She glanced at the clock. It was late morning. Ruby never slept in. George, seeing her open eyes, jumped off the bed and trotted to the camper door, dancing a little.

"I'm sorry, buddy. Hang on, I'll let you outside." She reached in the cabinet for a pair of yoga shorts. Pulling them on, she hurried to the door, running her hand through her tangles. It made her think of Joe's hands, buried deep in hair as his tongue explored her mouth.

George barked impatiently.

She opened the door just as Bill was passing her camper.

He glowered at her but murmured something. She was in such a good mood, she decided to take it as a good morning greeting.

"Good morning, Bill."

He turned back, surprised. Oops. Tactical error.

George lifted his leg and stared at Bill.

He showed his teeth. He liked doing that to Bill. It felt good.

He was beginning to not like doing that to Joe. He felt conflicted.

George turned and looked at Ruby expectedly.

"Come on, George. I'll feed you." She said loudly. "See you around, Bill," She threw over her shoulder as she let the dog back in the camper.

She filled George's dishes with fresh water and food then took a quick shower. She was surprised that Joe hadn't stopped by or texted her. After last night, she kind of expected it, but then they weren't teenagers. It was better anyhow. She really needed some time to think. She made a cup of coffee and thought about what to do for the day. The surf sounded quiet, so she decided she wanted to try to take her kayak in the ocean. The bay was fun, but she thought the ocean might be even better.

"Ya wanna go kayaking George?"

The dog jumped up wagging his tail. He spun in circles, clearly happy with Ruby's decision. Ruby gathered a couple of water bottles and her paddle leash, then the two of them went outside to take on the ocean.

After dragging her kayak across the beach, Ruby had worked up a sweat. George ran up and down the shore chasing birds, waiting for Ruby to get it together. She stowed the bottled waters and George's collapsible dish, then strapped on her life jacket. She whistled for her dog.

George came running, his ears happily flapping in the breeze. He was overcome with joy. Ruby felt a twinge of guilt thinking about what she had done last night and how George had been when she got home.

The little dog sat in front of her, his paw lifted. All had been forgiven. She bent down to put the dog's lifejacket on him, and he covered her face with happy licks. Impulsively, she hugged the dog to her.

"No matter what, George, I love you, first and foremost. Please don't forget that."

She wasn't sure if she was talking to the little dog or the memory of her deceased husband, but it really didn't matter. She needed it said. George looked into her eyes and she bowed her head. He raised his right foot to her, pawing her gently, drawing her close. He licked her earlobe, then spun around and jumped into the kayak, barking.

"Okay, okay. Enough mushy stuff. Let's go."

Ruby shoved off, and she settled down into the cockpit of the kayak. The waves were gentle, but it took some strength to paddle out. She wanted to get a little way off shore past the sandbar where small waves were breaking.

The sun warmed her muscles, and she paddled steadily out studying the water carefully. The sea was calm, and life was good. George was standing with his front paws on the deck of the kayak, tail wagging, obviously enjoying the ride.

Suddenly, his tail stopped, and he started barking excitedly. He looked over the starboard side of the kayak.

"Whoa, George. Don't throw your weight around or you'll dump us." Ruby compensated for the shift and looked where George was barking. There seemed to be a dark shape in the water, gliding just below the surface beside them.

Ruby felt her gut tighten. She knew sharks were common here, but she didn't think about them bothering her. Now she was beginning to wonder.

George barked louder. Ruby stopped paddling and watched the water beside her.

The shadow shot ahead then broke the surface of the water, it's gray back glistening in the sun.

A dolphin.

It dove again, then surfaced, a second one by its side.

Ruby laughed and started paddling. There was no way she

was going to be able to keep up with them. There was a soft splash next to her as a third dolphin surfaced. She realized she was surrounded by a pod which seemed to be keeping pace with her.

She leaned forward slightly and dug in with stronger paddle strokes. She was going to race them. She knew that she couldn't win, but it would be fun and great exercise. George kept shifting back and forth, keeping Ruby on her toes trying to keep the kayak upright. Before she knew it, Ruby had paddled a long way along the coastline. The dolphins slowly pulled away, leaving Ruby and George alone in the ocean.

"I guess it's about time we turn around and paddle the other way. What do ya say? Ready to head back, buddy?"

George wagged his tail and licked his chops pointedly.

"What's wrong? Are you thirsty?"

George woofed.

"Okay, hang on." Ruby dug into her deck bag and pulled out George's collapsible water dish. She placed it between her legs on the bottom of the kayak. George turned around facing Ruby and the bowl.

"Hey guy, give me room to work."

George's ears perked up. He looked over his shoulder. A lone jet ski was cutting through the waves, coming their way.

Ruby didn't notice.

She pulled a bottle of water out of the bag and poured some into George's bowl. He lapped it gratefully. Ruby sipped at the water remaining in the bottle. Hearing a whining sound, she looked up. A guy on a jet ski was heading their way.

George stopped drinking and growled.

Ruby took another pull from the bottle.

The sound was a lot louder now. Ruby focused on the jet ski.

It was heading right toward them.

"Asshole," Ruby murmured. It wasn't the first time a jet ski had played chicken with her. "Why do these people always like to swamp kayaks with their wakes? Hang on, George. This guy is an unmitigated jerk."

Ruby readied herself for the inevitable quick turn of the jet ski and the wave wash that would result.

"He'd better make the turn soon."

George growled loudly, then started barking.

The jet ski wasn't turning.

"Hey, asshole. Watch out." Ruby yelled, raising her paddle skyward, just in case the moron didn't see them.

The jet ski didn't slow or turn.

"Holy shit. Hang on. He is going to cut it close."

The jet ski bore down on them.

Just before it hit, Ruby saw his face.

Bill.

Chapter 36

George was thrown from the kayak. Salt water filled his nose and his eyes. He sneezed, trying to clear his airway. Instinct took over and he started to dog paddle, frantically reaching his paws forward, beating the water, and looking for anything to climb up on. He was wild with fear.

There was no solid ground, just water, lifting and falling in swells.

After a few minutes of desperate, exhausting thrashing, he realized that the life jacket held him high in the water. His panic started to ebb.

Ruby.

Where was Ruby?

George spun around, looking for his mistress. He didn't see her.

He heard the sound of the jet ski in the distance.

He still didn't see Ruby.

He whimpered, crying for his Ruby.

The kayak was upside down in the water, the ocean swells pushing it toward shore.

The dog spun again.

There she was.

Ruby was face up in the water, the life jacket doing its job. She wasn't moving. She rose and fell with the gentle swells, moving almost imperceptibly toward the beach.

George dog paddled toward her. Her paddle floated by her side attached to her lifejacket by the paddle leash. George took the leash in his mouth and turned toward shore.

He doggy-paddled as hard as he could.

His muscles were screaming, and it was hard to pant and breathe with the leash in his mouth.

After an eternity, his paws felt sand. The bottom.

The waves were small, almost gentle.

They helped him move his burden.

Ruby's back scraped the beach, and the forward movement stopped. George couldn't pull her any further.

He licked her face frantically. He didn't understand why she wouldn't move.

The small waves lapped around her.

Ruby was still.

George whined.

He didn't want to leave her.

She didn't move.

This part of the beach was isolated, devoid of people.

George licked her one more time and turned south, taking off at a dead run.

Chapter 37

J oe finished going through his latest online album. The pictures from the other day were good. The pictures of the south end of the island and the inland campsite looked great with the thunderstorm's darkened sky in the background. They looked positively wild. He was pleased.

He was even more pleased by the candid shot of Ruby, her head thrown back in laughter, her little dog licking her throat. Sea grass waved behind her auburn hair, and the dog's ears were lifted by the wind. It was an amazing shot.

Ruby.

He looked at his watch. It was early afternoon. He hadn't called her. He wanted her to have some time, figured she would need it to process everything that had happened the night before.

Would she come with him?

He kind of doubted it. He desperately wanted her to, but she didn't seem ready. The memory of her husband was too raw.

The dog didn't help either.

Damn him.

Joe laughed. Despite their differences, he liked the scrappy cur. He liked the fact that George would probably defend Ruby to his death. Joe liked that kind of dedication. He felt that way about Ruby, too. Could he make George understand that Ruby had room for the two of them in her life?

He scrolled through the pictures again, looking for the perfect wild inland scene to send his client. He was concentrating, trying to decide between two different photos, but something was distracting him.

He shook his head. He had to get this done. He examined the first one. The exposure was good, but the composition in the second was better.

What was nagging at him?

The second picture also had some great texture.

Barking.

And the lighting behind the sea grass was stunning.

Barking.

George.

Frantic barking.

Joe jumped up from picnic table.

He started toward the beach when a bedraggled frantic dog wearing a life jacket threw himself at Joe.

"George. What the hell?'

George barked, and whirled around.

"George, where's Ruby?"

George barked, and whirled again, running toward the beach.

Joe felt his stomach drop. Something was terribly wrong.

George looked like hell.

George turned and barked at him again, and Joe started running.

"How much further, buddy?"

Joe's legs were screaming from running in the beach sand. He had moved into the zone where the water was lapping the sand, giving him a more solid surface. He cursed himself. He was out of shape, and he was beginning to panic. *Where the hell was she?*

George barked at him, encouraging him to hurry. The dog's bark was getting raspy and quiet, his sides heaving with effort. He was limping slightly, but he pushed himself on.

In the distance, Joe saw a shape at the water's edge. It was blue and bright yellow.

Ruby's life jacket.

Joe kicked harder, faster, as did George.

They reached her at the same time.

George licked Ruby's face. Trying to wake her up.

Ruby didn't move.

George collapsed beside her, exhausted.

Chapter 38

The paramedics carried the litter across the dunes to the waiting ambulance. Joe followed, carrying George in his arms wrapped in a towel donated by a kind bystander. The desolate beach had filled with onlookers with the arrival of the ambulance. Another stranger had given Joe some water for himself and for the dog. George had gratefully lapped at the water poured in Joe's hand. Now he lay in Joe's arms, every part of his little body screaming in pain.

He whimpered for his Ruby.

Joe scratched his ears trying to soothe him.

"It's okay George. She's going to be okay. She was breathing. Thank God she was wearing a life jacket."

Joe followed the paramedics, frustrated because he couldn't answer any of their questions.

Where was she going?

Was she alone?

Was she on a boat?

That one he answered. He figured she had been out on her kayak, but he didn't see it anywhere. What had caused her to capsize? Why was she unconscious? What the hell had happened?

They barred Joe from ducking into the back of the ambulance with Ruby.

"I'm sorry, sir. We can't allow the dog. You can meet us at the hospital. It would really help if you could bring her ID, insurance cards, meds, lists of allergies, you know, the basics."

Joe nodded helplessly. Did Ruby have any allergies? Was she on any medications? He realized just how little he knew about this woman who had stolen his heart.

The park ranger offered Joe a ride back to his camper so he could get his truck. From there he would drive to Ruby's teardrop. He hoped he could get in.

Joe thanked the ranger when he dropped him at his campsite. Joe gathered George in his arms and carried him to his trailer, laying the dog on his bed as he got his wallet and truck keys. He picked up the exhausted dog again and gently placed him in the front seat of his truck. He ran to the driver's side of the truck and jumped in. His tires spun as he headed off to Ruby's trailer. George didn't even open his eyes.

As Joe drove down the camp road towards Ruby's trailer he was startled to hear the sleeping George growl, deep and threatening. Poor dog had been through a lot.

Joe looked up from the dog and swerved, just missing the truck pulling a trailer out of a campsite.

Asshole didn't even look. Pulled right in front of me. Go figure...the asshole is Bill. Well, good riddance, Joe thought. He was glad Ruby wasn't going to have to deal with that man anymore. Joe parked in front of Ruby's Jeep.

"Come on George. We're home." George opened one eye, sighed, then closed his eyes again. "I'm sorry buddy. I know you're tired." Joe reached across the seat and lifted the little dog into his arms.

Where would Ruby hide a key?

"George where is Ruby's spare key? Show me boy."

George looked at him from there he lay in his camp chair. Joe had placed him there when he had arrived. George had collapsed in the chair with a whimper.

"Why am I asking you. That only happens on TV."

George looked at him reproachfully.

"You're right, you brought me to Ruby. I can't ask for more."

Joe ran his hand under the lip edge of the trailer feeling for a spare key box. He didn't find any. He checked her box on the trailer tongue. It was locked. He felt underneath the box. Nothing.

Surely, she has a hidden spare key.

He looked at her little trailer again. Where would he hide a key if he were Ruby? He walked around the trailer again. Where would he…the refrigerator access panel. He turned the latch and the door sprung open. He reached inside and felt around the interior. Just when he was about to give up his fingers touched a small metal box. Bingo. He pulled the magnetic rectangle out of its hiding place and slide open the top. Nestled inside was a camper key.

"George, I found it," he announced to the dog. George thumped his tail weakly and watched with interest. Joe tried the key in the lock. The camper door opened.

He felt a little like he was violating Ruby, entering her camper without her, but he needed to find her wallet and snoop for medications.

George slid out of the chair, whimpering as he hit the ground. Stiffly he followed Joe into the camper.

Joe immediately saw Ruby's purse on the shelf above her bed. It was a small leather purse with a long strap. He was dumfounded. He had always noticed giant purses and wondered what kind of crap women felt the need to carry. He approved of this one, and it fit Ruby perfectly. He grabbed it and started to unzip it, then paused. Women's purses were sacred. George looked at him impatiently and barked softly.

Joe unzipped the purse.

He wasn't sure what he expected to find, but it wasn't mystical. There was a mini pack of tissues, lip balm, a set of keys, and a thin wallet. Joe pulled out the wallet and opened it.

He was confronted with the smiling face of Ruby's dead husband.

He knew it was George because the picture was from their wedding day. They were coming out of the church, laughing and ducking the spray of birdseed tossed by the well-wishers. Ruby was beautiful, her hair loose around her shoulders, her simple white wedding dress caught up in her right arm. She held hands with George.

He was a good-looking man, but not remarkable. Average height, average build, just pretty average, but George's smile couldn't have been any wider. It was obvious that this was the happiest man in the world enjoying the happiest moment of his life. His short life.

Joe felt a twinge in his gut. The love this man had for his new wife was palpable.

He turned his attention back to Ruby. She, too, was smiling, but there was something. He studied her face. It wasn't that she looked sad, or uncomfortable, or shy, or frightened. She was smiling and enjoying the joyous exit, but still…wait… that's what it was. It wasn't that there was something there in her face, it was that something was missing. That something was joy. She was not joyous on the occasion that should have been one of the most joyous of her life.

The dog whined softly.

Joe looked down.

The dog stared into Joe's eyes, then glanced at the picture in his hand.

He whimpered.

"I'm sorry," whispered Joe. "I am truly sorry." Then he felt stupid for saying that to the dog.

George reared up on his hind legs, wincing, and placed his front paws on Joe's thighs. He lifted his right foot and pawed Joe's forearm.

"You're right. We need to get going." Joe tucked the purse into his elbow and searched for medications. He went into the bathroom and checked the hanging toiletry bag. Nothing. He opened every cupboard and drawer, but still found nothing. That was it. He was going to assume Ruby didn't need any kind of prescription drug.

"Okay buddy. I've got to go. I want to take you with me, but it's too hot to leave you in the truck."

George hung his head for a minute, then turned and jumped up on Ruby's bed, laying down on his pillow with a sigh.

"I promise, I will come back for you, buddy. You won't spend the night alone."

Chapter 39

J oe left the hospital feeling lost. The only information the woman at the desk would give him was that Ruby had awakened briefly, but was now resting comfortably, and they were keeping her overnight for observation. She had only given him that because he produced her wallet and insurance card. She wouldn't let him in to see her because he wasn't family despite the fact that he wheedled, cajoled and tried to charm his way in.

He drove back to Ruby's trailer and inserted the key in the lock. The camper was quiet. George didn't growl or bark. That made Joe nervous. He reached in the open door and felt for a light switch. When he flipped it on, George lifted his head from his pillow, squinting. He licked his lips and blinked. His tail thumped weakly.

"Hey buddy." Joe said softly. "How ya feelin'?" The dog got up stiffly, then lay back down. "You're hurting' pretty badly, huh? How about I take you to my camper and put some heat on your sore muscles. It'll help you to feel better. First, I have to find your food."

George's ears perked up.

"Are you hungry?"

The dog's tail thumped harder on the bed.

"Okay, pal. I'll get you fixed up."

Joe looked around and found the dog's food and dishes. He also found a box of puppy biscuits and some jerky type treats. When Joe picked up the bag of jerky treats, George woofed.

"Here you go." Joe tossed a treat onto George's pillow. George made it disappear with remarkable speed. Joe walked over and scratched the dog's ears.

"Do me a favor, don't tell Ruby I fed you on the bed. I don't know if that is a permitted activity." Joe felt a tug in his heart. "George, there is so much I don't know, and I want to."

The dog crawled closer to him and licked his hand. Once again, the dog looked up and stared deeply into Joe's eyes. There was no growling from the dog, and his lip wasn't raised showing his teeth. There was just a look of sadness and extreme exhaustion.

"Don't worry, buddy. I won't hurt her. I promise."

The dog didn't break eye contact, as if weighing the strength of that promise. Then he flicked out his tongue again and licked Joe's hand, sealing the deal.

Joe found an empty grocery bag and loaded the dog's supplies. On an impulse he grabbed George's pillow. When he did, he saw Ruby's Ohio University shirt tucked under her pillow. He grabbed that, too.

When he reached his trailer, he fed George. While the dog was eating, he warmed a rice hot pad in his microwave. After he allowed the dog to relieve himself, Joe opened the camper door and placed the dog on the bed.

"Sorry buddy. My camper is a lot smaller than yours. The entire inside is bed, so it's you and me together. I hope you're not weirded out by that."

George looked around at the tiny interior then lay down on his pillow. Joe put Ruby's t-shirt next to the dog, who promptly rested his muzzle on the soft cotton fabric. Then Joe tested the temperature of the hot pack and then laid it against the little dog's back.

George sighed and thumped his tail. He smiled at Joe and promptly fell asleep.

Chapter 40

There was a far-off ringing sound, a buoy. The ocean. The air was heavy and wet. The buoy sounded closer. Joe felt that there was danger approaching. His face was washed with the ocean waves. Ruby. Where was she? He peered into the darkness, all the while trying to avoid the water splashing on his face. The buoy. He felt like he needed to get to the buoy. Ruby must be at the buoy.

Barking.

George.

He was lost in those waves.

He had to get him. He had to help. He had to get the water out of his mouth.

Joe's eyes flashed open just as George licked his tongue again.

"Argh…George…stop that. That's disgusting."

The dog barked.

The phone was ringing.

Joe reached out fumbling to grab the phone. He shook his head trying to clear the cobwebs and the remainder of the dream.

"Hello?"

"George. Where is George? Oh God, I don't know what I'll do…"

"Ruby, calm down… I—"

"Joe, please find George. I don't know what happened, but I don't know where he is. He would have been out all night, scared."

"RUBY. I HAVE GEORGE." Joe hated speaking firmly to her, but he had to get his message across to the frantic woman.

"You have him? Is he okay? Is he hurt?" She was still ramped up. He could hear the fear in her voice.

"Ruby, he's fine. He spent the night with me last night. He's been fed and he's hanging out with me, just us boys. When are they letting you go?"

"The doctor said I could go home. Thank you for taking care of George. How did you know? How did you get him? Would it be too much to ask for you to give me a ride?"

"Ruby, I'll be right there. Are you kidding? Do you know I was there last night, but they wouldn't let me in to see you? What happened to you? Why were you on the beach? Where was your kayak?"

"It's all really fuzzy. I remember kayaking and a jet ski was coming close to me. I think he hit me. I don't remember much after that. I think I remember floating and George was pulling me, but I'm not sure."

"It's okay. Don't worry about that. I'll be there as soon as I can, just hang tight."

"Okay. Are you sure George is okay?"

"He's fine. I will bring him with me so you can see for yourself."

"I don't think they'll let him in the hospital, and it's too hot in the car for him."

"Don't worry," said Joe. "Just let me take care of that. I will be there in a little bit."

Joe hung up the phone and looked at George.

George was sitting looking at Joe expectantly.

"So, do you want to come with me to go get Ruby?"

George jumped up wagging his tail and barked happily.

"It looks like you're feeling better, too. Hang on and I'll let you outside, then we'll go get your lady."

Joe pulled on his clothes, using the convoluted gymnastics required to dress in a tiny teardrop trailer. George seemed to be laughing at him. Joe pulled his shoes out of the bin under the trailer, slid them on, then stood up on the driveway. George jumped out, stretching as he hit the ground. He was still a little sore.

George took care of business while Joe made a big thermos of coffee. Then he grabbed his backpack out of the trailer.

"I'm going to have to sneak you into the hospital, so are you willing to ride in the backpack again?" George curled his lip at Joe but wagged his tail at the same time.

"I didn't say you had to like it. Come on, jump into the truck."

George sat down and looked at Joe. His ears were hanging limply, and he held up a paw.

"Still too sore to jump in the truck, huh? Okay, hang on. Joe reached down and lifted George carefully, placing him on the seat. With as much dignity as possible, George sat looking out the front window and waited patiently for Joe to get in on the other side and get this show on the road.

Chapter 41

"Hey you." Joe slipped through the hospital room door and kissed Ruby on the forehead. She was sitting in a chair next to the bed. He looked her over carefully. She was pale, and she had a scrape on her forehead, a good size knot underneath the wound. She still looked beautiful despite her tangled hair and her bruised face.

"Hey. Wait. Where's George? It's too hot in the car for him"

"Shhhh." Joe placed his finger gently on Ruby's lips. He closed the door to the room and pulled the curtain around for good measure.

He pulled the backpack off his shoulder and unzipped the top. George pushed his black nose through the ever-widening opening, then burst out and onto Ruby's lap, covering her with kisses.

"Easy, George. Don't hurt her," said Joe, alarmed.

"I'm fine. I am so happy to see him. He can kiss me all he wants!"

Ruby wrapped her arms around her dog and held him

close. She buried her nose in his fur while tears slipped from her eyes.

"I think George saved my life. I think he got me to the beach. I don't know how a little dog like him managed to do it, but I know he did."

George wiggled his butt, wagging his tail as fast as he could. He wagged so hard he lost his balance and almost fell off of Ruby's lap. Joe reached out and shoved the dog back up to a more stable position.

The room door open and the curtains were pushed aside.

"Ruby, I have your release…is that a dog?"

"Why yes, I believe it is," said Ruby, laughing.

"Let me rephrase that," the efficient looking nurse in the white scrubs said. "Why is there a dog in this room?"

"He has come to take me home. Doesn't everyone's dog do that?" Ruby's eyes sparkled with mirth. At that moment, Joe knew she was going to be just fine.

"No, they don't. I don't know how you managed to get that dog in here, young man, but you need to take him back out."

"Backpack," said Joe

"No, back out."

"No, backpack. I brought him in my backpack."

Ruby was doubled over laughing at the look on the nurse's face.

"Well you can stuff him back in there and march him right back out. Along with his sassy mistress!" The nurse was smiling as she said it. She pulled the curtain back around so the view from the hall was blocked. Then she proceeded to scratch George's ears as she gave Ruby her going home instructions.

"Don't worry, ma'am. I will make sure she gets plenty of rest, and I will definitely keep her out of trouble."

Joe walked behind the nurse as she wheeled Ruby to the door of the hospital. She waited with Ruby while Joe got his truck. George sat in Ruby's lap waiting, too.

Chapter 42

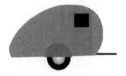

R uby, George, and Joe sat on the beach at the water's edge watching dusk settle over the ocean. Dolphins played in the surf while sea birds cried overhead. Plovers ran through the lapping water snagging a meal. It was peaceful and calm. A perfect night for inner turmoil.

"Have you thought about coming with me?" Joe asked, running his thumb across the top of her hand resting on his thigh.

Ruby sighed.

George looked up at her.

"Yes, I have thought about it. I just don't know. What time do you leave tomorrow?"

"I want to be on the road by nine. Ruby, there's no pressure. I want you to come. I don't want this to be goodbye, but I also understand and respect your side of this. It's too early. You don't know me well. I get it."

"Joe, I didn't ask to be turned free, but my husband died and gave me the chance to live my dream of adventure. I'm not sure I'm ready to give that up yet."

George laid down between the two of them, his head resting on top of their clasped hands.

"Okay. You have one more day here before your reservation runs out. Stay. Think about it. I will text you the address. If you decide to come, then just come. Text me if you are on your way, and I can make sure you have a place to park your trailer. Just think about it."

The dusk turned to dark, and they still sat there lost in their own thoughts. Later, Joe walked the two of them to Ruby's trailer and kissed her goodbye. She returned the kiss. George jumped up in his camp chair and sat looking over the dunes.

Joe walked away, his hands in his pockets, his head down.

Ruby called George to her trailer.

She went to bed, tears running down her cheeks.

George snuggled up to her and licked away the tears. He sighed and snuggled up to her. They both felt a little lost.

In the morning, Ruby took a shower and tried to work on her editing assignment. George was restless, pacing the camper.

"Lay down, George. I can't concentrate."

George looked at her, hurt, but laid down for a few minutes. Then he started scratching his armpit, his back paw thudding on the camper floor at the end of each scratch.

"Damn it George, stop it."

George stopped and stared at Ruby.

"I'm sorry. Oh geez, I'm sorry George. Would you like to go for a walk down the beach? We'll get some exercise, and I'll work when I get back. Deal?"

George jumped up and happily wagged his tail. Ruby grabbed a bottle of water and pulled her still wet hair through the back of an Indians baseball cap.

Together they walked through the dunes to the beach. The beach was quiet except for a few families and a couple flying a kite shaped like a shark. They looked happy as they looked up in the sky holding hands.

Ruby's heart twisted. She had been trying to ignore the empty gnawing feeling in her gut. She knew Joe had left. It was already nine-forty-five. He was probably already in Virginia by now.

She and George wandered in between the dunes and ended up at Joe's trailer space. The spot was deserted. Void. Empty, like her heart.

George looked up at her and whined. He reared up on his hind legs and pressed her thighs with his front paws. She leaned down and he licked her face, cleaning the tears.

"Come on, George. I have work to do."

Together they walked back to Ruby's teardrop.

Chapter 43

R uby finished her editing then drove to a nearby market. She wandered through, looking at her choices for dinner. Nothing sounded good. Her mind flashed back on the first meal with Joe, the mussels and clams they had collected. It was nice to share food with someone again. She really didn't want to eat alone.

She wasn't alone, she reminded herself. She had George.

She couldn't do this to herself. This is the life she had wanted. She straightened her shoulders. *Quit feeling sorry for your-self. This was your choice.* Determined to have a nice meal, she bought some shrimp and a pound of pasta, some nice French bread and salad fixings, and added some more treats for George. George would share her meal. She wouldn't be alone.

Back at the camper, Ruby set the pot of water on to boil. She melted some butter in a frying pan and cleaned the shrimp. After adding oil and salt to the boiling water, she dropped the pasta in, stirring it so it wouldn't stick.

"I have just enough time to make a mojito," Ruby announced to George. He wagged his tail and sat up.

"You can have a treat when we sit down for dinner. Here, have some fresh water."

She quickly fixed her drink while stirring the pasta and sautéing the shrimp. She added a generous sprinkling of Cajun seasonings to the shrimp and made herself a small tossed salad. When the pasta was ready, she tossed it with the sautéed Cajun shrimp.

Ruby went outside and covered her picnic table with her flamingo table cloth. She liked the retro look, and it always made her happy. After a couple of trips, her dinner and drink were at the table. George joined her, and they ate together facing the dunes, enjoying the fresh breeze and the sound of the waves on the beach.

It was perfect.

Almost.

Ruby set down her fork.

"George, I'm unhappy. What do I do? I just don't know what to do."

Follow your heart.

Ruby looked down at her cell phone. There was a text from Joe.

Follow your heart.

George put his paw on the cell phone and stared at Ruby, his liquid brown eyes boring into her soul.

"What if I don't know my heart. George?"

Ruby pushed her plate aside, crossing her arms on the picnic table and dropping her head. She cried softly, hating herself for her weakness.

George put his front paws on her shoulders and nuzzled her hair, whining softly. When she didn't move, he patiently sat next to her, his paw on her thigh, and he waited. He knew she would figure it out soon. He knew she would listen to her heart.

Chapter 44

"Come on, George, get in the Jeep. We have a long drive ahead of us."

Ruby's pony tail whipped around, and she looked behind her for her dog.

"Do you want to go to Florida or not?"

George came running from the back of the trailer with a Frisbee in his mouth.

"Where did you steal that from?" laughed Ruby as the dog streaked past her and jumped into the front seat. He put his front paws on the dashboard, the Frisbee hanging from one tooth, and smiled comically. His tail was wagging, and he was ready to go.

"Are you ready for the next adventure, George?" The dog panted happily at his lady, dropping the Frisbee on the floor.

"Okay buddy let's go find Joe."

Turn the page for a sneak peek at
the next book in this series!

Teardrops and Rest Stops

LARK GRIFFING

Chapter 1

Joe cruised over the causeway leaving Assateague Island and Ruby behind. He glanced in the rearview mirror. The little teardrop trailer he pulled traveled smoothly behind his truck. Everything was well. Except it wasn't. Ruby wasn't following him. Not that he expected it. He had only known that amazing women for a few days, but he had hoped she would take him up on the adventure.

He wasn't going to give up.

He turned on the GPS and started the course he had set up the night before. The Florida Keys. He had a client who wanted his hotel photographed for an upcoming marketing campaign. Joe had been looking forward to the job. He loved the Keys and he was planning on doing some fishing and shooting some photographs to bulk up his stock photo portfolio. Now he wasn't as excited about it. He was going to be alone.

He had been alone for the past eight months, ever since his fiancé broke up with him to run off wth a body builder. He had been bitter, angry, and bewildered. Then he met Ruby. Now, all he felt was alone and that he was missing something, and that something was her. And her little dog. Her annoying, protective, jealous reincarnated husband of a little dog, George.

Joe laughed thinking about the first time he thought the damn dog was Ruby's husband come back to life in the body of a dog. It was an insane idea. Ludicrous, and he knew it. But the damn dog knew what he was thinking and even got in the way when Joe tried to make a move on Ruby. Damn dog. On the other hand, that damn dog had saved her life, and Joe would never forget it.

Eight hours later he pulled into Santee State Park in South Carolina. He had reservations for the night. He backed his little teardrop camper into his site and crawled inside to his bed. It was still early, but he was tired. He had a sandwich he picked up earlier, so he flipped up the side table attached to his door and put the sandwich on it.

He wasn't hungry.

He stared at his cell phone, willing it to give him some indication that Ruby might be thinking about him. There was nothing.

What did he expect? He just met the woman.

But still.

His fingers hovered over the screen.

Text her.

He shook his head at himself.

Just text her. Let her know that you are thinking about her.

He sighed.

He unwrapped his sandwich and took a bite.

I wonder what she is having for dinner. I wonder if she is eating alone. Maybe a friendly neighbor asked to join her. After all, that's how this all got started.

He pulled up her last text. His fingers hesitated.

Just let her know she is on your mind. No pressure. Just a friendly thought.

He took another bite of his sandwich. It was a lonely bite. No Ruby. No George to try to win over with a morsel or two.

His fingers tapped on his phone.

Follow your heart.

Joe hit send.

Chapter 2

R uby stared down at the text on her phone. It was the umpteenth time in two days that she had looked at it. *Follow your heart.* It's what her husband told her when he died. It's what a friend had told her when she was so lost she didn't know where to turn. It was the phrase that had come to her in her sleep. *Follow your heart.*

But did she know her heart? She thought she did. She always wanted to be wild and free, exploring and having non-stop adventures.

She had put that dream aside when she had married George. Dear, sweet George. Solid and steadfast. An accountant. A planner. A man who loved his recliner and his losing Cleveland sports teams. George. The man who knew her heart even when she thought he didn't. The man who knew he was going to die, so he secretly bought Ruby her teardrop camper, so she could follow her impetuous dream. The man with the foresight to provide her with an insurance policy that would provide her with enough funds to keep her comfortable. Dear, sweet George. Dear, dead George.

Now that she was free, she fiercely wished she wasn't. She would trade it all to have her George back.

A tear meandered down her cheek, ending in the corner of her mouth. Salty.

George gently licked it away.

George, the dog. Not George, the husband.

She reached over and scratch the little Border Terrier mix behind the ears. He stretched his neck out and smiled, his eyes half closed.

George had come to her at a national forest campsite. He was a dirty stray, and she was alone. She cleaned him up, discovering a leather collar with the name *George* embossed in the leather.

That threw Ruby. She didn't want to have anything to do with the dog, but a kind forest ranger and the persistent pup had convinced Ruby to take a chance on the mutt. Now, they were inseparable.

George had very strong opinions on men. Most of them he didn't like. He had raised his lip and snarled at Joe on many occasions.

Joe just laughed at him.

George let Joe know he wasn't amused.

Joe became uneasy when he realized the dog could read his mind. But he really couldn't. Could he?

Joe joked that George, the husband had come back reincarnated as George, the dog. Joe laughed about that, uneasily. It was just too strange.

Ruby was heading down to the Florida keys, pulling her little teardrop camper. She was traveling toward Joe, but he didn't know it. She wasn't in a hurry. She was taking her time. Thinking.

They had just met. She wasn't ready for a relationship. She still missed her husband. She liked being free and alone, but she didn't always like being alone. She was conflicted.

She had George.

She was still lonely.

She drove toward Florida.

Somewhere in Georgia her phone rang. It was her boss, Laney. She wanted to let Ruby know that the article about Assateague Island was great and they had selected some of Joe's photos to accompany it. She also had several more articles that needed Ruby's editing skills, and Ruby would find them in her inbox. Mostly Laney was nosey and wanted to know if Ruby was alright and what was up with this Joe guy. Was he just a professional contact, or was there something there?

Ruby deflected most of the questions, but Laney was good and when they hung up, Laney was reminding her that Ruby had a lot of life ahead of her and it was okay to consider relationships. Ruby ignored the hint.

The Jeep rolled south, pulling the trailer steadily, getting ever closer to the Florida Keys. Ruby had no idea where Joe was staying. She wasn't ready to find out. She wanted to discover the Keys on her own terms. If Joe was still around when she was ready to share the discovery, then so be it. If not, it was never meant to be.

Sign up for Lark's newsletter

Would you like to know when Lark releases her next book? Do you want a sneak peek at sample chapters? If so, sign up for Lark Griffing's newsletter.

Subscribe now

Or use this URL to subscribe

http://eepurl.com/dH1mzz

Acknowledgments

There are a lot of people who help me get a book ready for publication. Without them, I wouldn't have the finished product you see.

First, I want to thank my editor, J.C. Wing of Wing Family Editing. She not only finds all of my grammar and punctuation mistakes, she is my champion and my cheerleader. She is always encouraging and kind.

Next, I want to give a big thank you to all the people in the teardrop world who helped guide us on our journey in our teardrop camper. Those evenings around the campfire with the Tearjerkers are always inspiring!

I also want to thank my advance readers, Kimi and Tracy. I couldn't do it without you. You guys are my final reality check. Thanks for the wonderful support and the quick turn around. Those all-nighters you pull are priceless!

And as always, I want to thank my husband, Joe and my youngest son, Charlie for allowing me to insist they stop what they are doing to read a passage or a story. They are the ones who hold me up and keep me going. Without them, I have nothing.

Also by Lark Griffing

Young adult novels:

The Last Time I Checked I Was Still Here
The Starfish Talisman

Short Story Collections

Dog on the Doorstep
Twelve Tales A'Telling

About the Author

Lark Griffing likes to bring her sense of adventure to her writing. Her first two novels are young adult; *The Last Time I Checked, I Was Still Here*, a coming of age story and *The Starfish Talisman*, an old-fashioned ghost story.

Dog on the Doorstep is Lark's collection of short stories and flash fiction for the holiday season about hope and the love of pets. She is also a contributor to the short story anthology *Twelve Tales A-Telling: a Modern Twist on a Holiday Classic.*

Teardrops and Flip Flops is the first novel of her new romantic comedy series, A Gone to the Dogs Camper Romance.

Lark collects hobbies like some people collect friends. When not writing and teaching, she is hiking, kayaking, SCUBA diving, camping, and enjoying life to the fullest with her family. She is married to a wonderful man and has two sons. She also shares her home with a precocious golden doodle, Maggie and a tabby cat, Dickens.

Keep up with Lark at her website:

www.LarkGriffing.com

facebook.com/larkgriffing

twitter.com/Lark_Griffing

instagram.com/LarkGriffing

Made in the USA
Columbia, SC
21 April 2021

36586831R00138